THE REST IS HISTORY

i

ii

THE REST IS HISTORY

Part one

Ali Nelson

iv

THE REST IS HISTORY

For Adele, Jake and family.

Trafalgar, Technology and the Toilet.

Tunnels, Tunes and the Trombone.

Toffs, Tasks and the Trumpet.

Chapter 1

Sophie lay on the bed; still. As her mind ticked over, analysing her surroundings everything seemed to be in order and yet somehow it felt different. Not that she was too bothered, juggling college and a full time job had become spectacularly challenging of late and frankly she was glad of the rest. Coping with coursework was hard enough, but also contending with the inefficiencies of her grumpy boss required a certain level of diplomacy and a quick wit - luckily Sophie had both.

These attributes, along with a very over active imagination were constantly employed as a defence mechanism against the mundane – typically her mind was filled with a frenetic buzz of ideas, images, music, that pulsated through her head in the same way that tube trains scream round the underground network during rush hour. It was into this secret labyrinth that she would withdraw, escaping from reality at a moment's notice, affording her time and space to explore the limits of her imagination and more importantly, to refresh the soul.

The usual cause behind these surreal excursions was Bob Marsh, her employer; he seemed to go through life rowing like crazy but with both oars out the water; it was because of this their relationship had been built on a foundation of tension held together by friction - with daily, sometimes hourly battles between Bob`s outdated views and her sanity. Sophie never really understood the rationale behind her loyalty; the boss was rude to punters, incompetent beyond comprehension and slightly hard of understanding but, despite all these traits she felt compelled to keep turning up for her shifts and support him through good and bad.

`Caramel Two` rehearsal studios had been purchased by Bob ten years earlier after he was forced to take early retirement from his post on the council. The seller had successfully persuaded him it was a thriving business and that he had the right attributes to build up an agreeable nest egg. In reality, Bob, having worked as a pen pusher for most of his life, was clueless about most things outside of co-ordinating refuse collection - really he wasn't very good at that either.

Having no business acumen whatsoever didn't deter him in the slightest; Bob convinced himself he could make up for the lack of commercial experience with boundless enthusiasm and charisma - from the start he took to the role of entrepreneur like a duck to custard, and it didn't take him long to realise he hated loud music and the people who created it. Clearly his children's inheritance had been well and truly squandered. Despite the quirky nature of Bob's acquisition, through grit, determination and controlled ineptitude he launched `Caramel Two` and over the next decade the good ship bounced off rocks, floundered on hidden sandbanks, and weathered lashing storms as it merely sat in dry docks waiting for a lick of paint.

Despite all their disagreements and Bob's constant moaning to Sophie about money, the wife, and how the wife spends the money, he was actually well disposed towards his `trainee` and (in his mind at least), had taken her under his wing to impart the full benefit of his years of wisdom. Sophie sort of appreciated this, but at times it made telling him to sod off, slightly more awkward. Recently she had set up a function band with a view to providing music for the lucrative corporate market and Bob volunteered his services as their business manager, despite them not actually looking for one. He promised to promote gigs and help run the band, but in reality he was simply the `ninth Beatle` as one of them put it. No matter how she looked at it, Sophie was faced with the fact that Bob was her boss - twice over.

* * *

As she lay there pondering, Sophie's imagination suddenly sparked, sending her off into a visionary cul-de-sac.

"I wonder if I could re-paint some of the world's classic paintings, but from a different view point?" she mused. Even as the last words of this surreal question were still rattling around the deepest recesses of her mind, a vivid image of the back of the Mona Lisa's head lit up her imagination. "Hmmm...something's missing..." She expanded the profile in her mind's eye to reveal Da Vinci loitering around in the background, standing at an easel trying to encourage a smile from his subject. Sophie smiled - it was little excursions like this, into her slightly odd, internal world that got her through the day.

At this time Sophie wasn't actually asleep so she hit the over-ride button in her brain and her thoughts became more realigned with reality; a history assignment was looming and she really should revise. Covering more and more shifts at the studios had started to affect her studies and she was falling behind, but now was the perfect time to catch up.

"What were we supposed to be looking at?" she quizzed herself - her cluttered mind had become a little fogged up. As she sorted through the filing system in her head, looking for inspiration a voice was suddenly projected over her internal PA system.

"The Battle of Trafalgar." it proclaimed. The disconnected voice was friendly and familiar, one that had given her help and advice on many occasions.

"Oh, yes. Trafalgar." Sophie found the correct folder in her mind's archive and started with the basics.

"Twenty-first October, eighteen-o-five. Yup - got that. What else? The Georgian navy, Nelson, Hardy, Collingwood..." Her mind had begun to wander - Leonardo Da Vinci had now morphed into Groucho Marks and was conducting an invisible orchestra with his cigar.

"Concentrate!" she chastised herself, half annoyed that her attention had been interrupted, half amused at Da Vinci's transition. She made a conscious effort to get back on track.

"Hang on, what was it Mr. Johnson said? - Always place yourself within a historical context to have an affinity with the people involved." Johnson was Sophie's college tutor whom she had taken a liking to from his very first lecture. Luckily for her he was also a keen guitarist and often used the studios to rehearse with his duo; her guilty pleasure was to see him away from the regime of the college. Sophie re-focused her mind.

"HMS Victory..." She paused to mull over her lecturer's advice. "I wonder what it was really like to have been on board during the battle. I should check it out."

Although not fully compos-mentis, Sophie slid off the bed and shuffled over to the door. She paused and listened. Nothing.

"Come on brain, don't let me down now." When she didn't want bizarre thoughts they relentlessly cascaded out of her mind, now when they would actually be useful, all her grey matter could muster was a blue circle, spinning clockwise.

"I wonder what would have happened if the RAF had the Millennium Falcon during World War Two?" She forced this bizarre thought through her mind in an attempt to crank the starting handle of her imagination. It worked! Sophie could sense the mechanism of her mind slowly but surely start to turn, heaving under a massive strain in the same way a mighty steam engine builds up enough power to find traction to make forward momentum possible. Suddenly, from the other side of the wall the sound of crashing waves could be heard. Tilting her head slightly, as if to get a second opinion from a different angle, she listened again. After further concentrated eavesdropping, Sophie could just about make out muffled commands being bellowed - the words having only just been dispatched were being carried away by the winds that charged over open waters. Although barely audible, Sophie could tell by the tone and delivery the words were meant as directives and recipients probably should obey them without question. As a large smile crept across her face, suddenly she felt the floor move.

"Earthquake!?" she said out loud. The floor rocked back to the original position, then tilted again; there was a certain rhythm to its movement. Sophie paused to take in what was happening; glancing around the swaying room she noticed a mahogany framed mirror which wasn't present before...Full of curiosity, she staggered towards it - hampered by the ever moving floor.

Having reached the heavy-set mirror she brushed off a thick layer of dust from its surface and gazed hard at the reflection expecting to see a sleepy Sophie staring back at her; instead she was confronted by a totally overwhelming view. There stood before her was Vice Admiral, Horatio Nelson - well, it was herself, but dressed as the famous naval commander.

Sophie let a few moments pass, enough to comprehend the situation - knowing how her brain worked she convinced herself this was nothing more than a revision session for a history test, albeit a slightly bizarre one. As the image of this national hero reflected back at her, Sophie felt a great sense of pride began to well up inside; she pompously adjusted her battle coat, straightened her sword in its sheath, turned around...and promptly threw up. The swell of the room had become more pronounced.

"Ok, not pride; sea sickness!" she mumbled, remembering this was a malady Nelson suffered from. Sophie made her way cautiously back across the room; as she reached the door, without hesitating she opened it and peered through.

* * *

The adjacent room was obviously part of a ship - it also rocked with a similar motion to the bedroom. The decoration was quite elaborate from what Sophie could make out; only a handful of oil burners shed a faint light across the area and the air that hit her nostrils was damp with a hint of smoke from the lights. Straining her eyes to examine the surroundings, all Sophie could see was wood everywhere; floor, ceiling and walls. A small coat of arms that hung near a window caught her eye and she went over to examine the plaque underneath; inscribed in ornate writing was the ships name. HMS Victory!

"I'm on the Victory!" she exclaimed. "I'm on the bloody Victory!" She fizzed with excitement, her mind raced way ahead exploring all the possibilities that this situation could bring. Then she paused. Studying the past was a passion for Sophie, and now with first-hand experience it felt tangible, but she also was humbled by the significance of her position; with this privilege came responsibility - the weight of history could bear down and overwhelm her at any time...

Sophie's deep thoughts were disturbed by the general melee from outside which had suddenly became much louder and very real; through a window to her right she became aware of an increase in commotion, men in uniforms shouting at other men in not quite so nice uniforms.

"They must be prepping for battle." she said out loud. At this point Sophie had a feeling of diligence towards her studies and realised this was a fantastic opportunity not to be missed. She moved not but two steps towards the action when out of the shadows stepped a figure dressed in period clothes, not too dissimilar to herself.

"There you are, My Lord." he bellowed. The man was over six foot tall and had trouble standing upright in the confined area. Her initial thoughts were he was in the wrong job, but her roving mind was bought back into focus quickly as she realised this was a massive case of mistaken identity. Her brain started to compute all the possible scenarios of how this was going to play out. Shuffling her feet anxiously, she stared at the floorboards.

"Hang on a mo." she thought. "I'm just on a history field trip - I'm in charge. My dream; my rules!" Her course notes came flooding back into her consciousness and she decided to take action - lead from the front. After all, she was Nelson!

"Ah, Captain Hardy!" she said, taking an educated guess; Sophie recalled from a distant lecture, he was a man of large stature. "Step forward man." As ordered, he moved out of the gloom and into an area, slightly less gloomy. Sophie recognised him instantly...Mr. Johnson. Her imagination was helpfully filling in characters for her by using people she knew from reality; considering she didn't have a clue what Nelson's commander looked like anyway, this seemed like a good plan. She took a deep breath, held it for a few seconds then let rip.

"The enemy has been sighted on the horizon and we stand on the brink of an historic battle. I want to send a message to Collingwood and the rest of the fleet. Something inspirational." This coherent and fairly historically accurate outburst even took Sophie by surprise, but she was pleased with it as an opening gambit. Johnson thought for a brief moment before replying.

"Your country needs you?" he volunteered.

"Sounds a bit avant-garde." responded Sophie.

"What about; we'll fight them on the beaches?" Sophie stalled - was Mr. Johnson testing her historical knowledge or simply her imagination just playing around with facts in its usual, abstract manner? She decided to go with the obvious.

"We're not going near any bloody beaches!" The officer didn't react, after all he was addressing a superior. Sophie continued. "It needs to be a rallying call to arms - to motivate the crew. Send this to all hands." She cleared her throat. "England expects every man will do his duty." She delivered the famous edict with the clarity and precision of a Shakespearian actor.

"Right-ho," said Johnson, possibly a bit too cheerfully considering the magnitude of the occasion. He then removed a mobile phone from his inside jacket pocket and whilst mouthing the words just issued to him, composed a text message.

"Hardy, what are you doing?" Sophie was slightly bemused by this behaviour.

"Sending your message, my Lord. I took the liberty of adding a smiley face."

Sophie was now struggling to keep her thoughts together; was Johnson impersonating Hardy, or was it actually Hardy taking on the form of Johnson? But surely - this was all in her mind anyway? It didn't overly bother her, she was enjoying the juxtaposition of fiction and historical fact combined with a hint of twisted logic. However, the conversation did need to come back round to some sort of relevance.

"What happened to signalling with the flags, and all that?" she asked, throwing in a nautical reference.

"Went out with the Ark, my Lord," retorted Johnson, throwing in a biblical reference.

The next occurrence *really* threw a curve ball at Sophie, even by her standard. The door leading from the quarter deck burst open and Bob rushed in clutching a piece of paper, he was dressed in scruffy, ill- fitting clothes and obviously held no position of authority aboard the Victory.

"Urgent fax for you, Sir!" He handed the memo to Sophie while gasping for breath having just sprinted the length of the ship.

"Sir?" she mused. "Hang on, my boss just called me, Sir! This is going to be fun!" Her thoughts were suddenly interrupted by a voice from across the room.

"When are you chaps going to get on email?" it said from within the woody darkness. Sophie spun around to identify who spoke. The glow of the oil lamps were now being augmented by the glow of a lap top screen, in which the owners face was illuminated. Sophie recognised him to be the lad from Johnson`s duo; a drummer who was always with him at the studio. However, currently dressed as Nelson`s private secretary, he was now seated at a desk in the middle of the Victory`s wardroom, frantically typing away. The whole scene threw Sophie`s mind out of kilter - twenty first century technology, on board the Georgian Navy`s finest ship of the line; recognisable people from day to day environs dressed as historical characters... As she stood there, mind buffering like an over-worked PC, Johnson reached across, took the fax from her and began to read...

"My Lord, the GPS tracking has put our estimated destination of engagement at the Cape of Trafalgar. Is this OK?" He paused and waited for confirmation. Sophie continued trying to compute all the information in the scene before her, but was struggling.

"ETA is around twelve noon." he helpfully added. "The weather centre has also issued a storm warning for the next forty eight hours." Sophie blinked, but said nothing - Johnson cleared his throat and carried on.

"And, it says here the guitar amp in studio `A` is broken." He paused - this time Sophie remembered she had the power of speech, but from her vast vocabulary, found only one word.

"Pardon?"

Johnson again cleared his throat and repeated the message.

"The amp in studio `A` is broken." Sophie spoke once more, this time finding another word.

"What?"

She blinked again. Suddenly it felt like the forward motion of time had been subjected to heavy braking; everything slowed to a fraction of its normal tempo - the lids of her eyes felt like an invisible force were dragging them slowly down. Lethargically they closed, landing with a weighty thud which sent a mini shock-wave rippling towards her cheek bones. There they sat, shrouding her pupils` waiting for the upward, return journey. Sophie`s breathing had also slowed in relation to the timeframe and she could sense every single pulse that pumped round her body. This strange sensation carried on for what seemed like an eternity, but all she could do was wait for something to happen...

Slowly her eye lids broke free and began to rise - a bright light flooded through the narrow opening, hitting her pupils as they fought to re-adjust to their surroundings. Disorientated, she froze to the spot.

* * *

It took a brief moment for all of Sophie`s senses to re-focus their respective traits and work together to find out where she was. Quite quickly it become apparent that she was no longer at sea.

Was she ever?

The smell of wood had been replaced by the smell of carpet, the damp had now gone from her nose, her ears weren`t detecting crashing waves any more - Sophie strained to identify what the noise was, although barely audible it was familiar but the turmoil in her head prevented the sound-waves from being interpreted efficiently. Her eyes began to regain more focus, so she started by looking down at herself – Nelson`s uniform had been replaced by normal, everyday attire.

Clarity had now returned to her ears and she instantly recognised the subdued sounds that flowed in her direction – the unmistakable guitar riff of `Sweet Child of Mine` was being played using most of the right notes. Sophie`s mind, while still spinning, was interrupted by another noise; an attention seeking polite, but obvious cough. Her eyes refocused and brain sharpened up - she was back behind the desk in the reception of `Caramel Two` studios. Reality hit her and she groaned finding one more word from her vocab.

"Bugger!" she muttered. The throat clearing continued followed by a familiar proclamation.

"The guitar amp in studio `A` is broken." Mr. Johnson stood in front of Sophie, calmly reiterating the problem. He too was now dressed as one would normally dress for a Tuesday evening. Blushing, Sophie got herself together, scanned around the room for reassurance of the environment, but more importantly to check the boss hadn't noticed she had been daydreaming. Bob, as usual was nowhere to be seen - Knobby had also vanished from sight. She relaxed.

"So sorry, Mr. J. I was miles away." Technically she had been; Sophie hated lies, so chose her words carefully.

"Anywhere nice?" he joked.

"Battle of Trafalgar." As soon as Sophie spoke she knew this would make no sense to anyone outside her head. "I was mentally revising for that history exam." she hurriedly added.

"Got it." he smiled. "How`s it going?"

"Ok..." Sophie paused. "Did they have mobile phones back then?" Her internal wiring had become crossed and the lines between the two worlds blurred. Momentarily Johnson stood there looking slightly perplexed, but eventually decided she was joking so moved the conversation along.

"The amp in our studio...."

"Yes of course." Sophie interrupted him. "I`ll get the boss to pop in and sort it for you." Johnson`s demeanour changed instantly.

"I hope the grumpy sod is in a better mood today?" Sophie always knew of a friction between Bob and her tutor but never really understood why.

"I doubt it; his birthday was yesterday and no-one remembered." She responded.

"That's a pity, I wish I'd known..." Sophie was a little taken aback by this sudden appearance of affection from Johnson towards Bob - standard protocol was to fire off a volley of contempt to score points, even if one of them was absent. "I think I would have liked the opportunity to *not* get him a card."

Sophie smiled weakly as she recognised normal service had been resumed. Being diplomatic she returned to the original topic of conversation.

"I will get the amp sorted out soonest." she said reaching for her mobile. Johnson thanked her as he walked back down the corridor.

* * *

The door to the rear of the reception area came swinging open with force and Bob rushed through, exactly in the same manner as he entered the wardroom on the Victory; still dressed scruffily, but this time in modern attire. Sophie had an acute feeling of daja vu...

"Didn't this just happen a moment ago; in the nineteenth century?" she mumbled to herself.

"Beg your pardon?" barked Bob.

"There you are, I was just about to phone you."

"I only live upstairs - why didn't you just come and get me?" He demanded. Sophie expected this logic from someone of that generation but felt the need to defend her younger view point.

"This is so much quicker." She said waving the phone at him. "I wish you had some modern tech."

"I don't like new-fangled equipment." He responded, preserving the right to be a moany old git. "I just don't get it!" Sophie opened her mouth to respond but didn't have a chance as Bob continued.

"I really believe that mobile phones are killing the art of conversation." Sophie stared vacantly as the rant continued. "Why don't they make things like the old days? Simple, but reliable. Built to last!"

"Apparently one of your simple, but reliable, built to last amps has just blown up." Sophie dismantled Bob`s argument with a few, well-chosen words. "Mr. Johnson is complaining."

"Johnson! He's always complaining." Bob dismissed this information - if it were anyone else he would have feigned interest. "I'll sort him out in a mo - anything else?" he asked, changing the subject. Sophie went for broke.

"A pay rise would be nice."

"Dream on." said Bob, not knowing how accurate this statement was.

"You`re so tight!" Sophie was becoming frustrated.

"Every penny counts, young lady. I`ve just had to order a new piano for the live room and now it looks like Johnson has knackered more equipment..." Sophie knew what was coming next. "... plus, I've got spouse related, financial issues." And there it was; whenever Bob was moaning about cash the conversation inevitably ended up with him complaining about his wife.

"Mrs. Marsh been spending again?" A pointless question - Sophie already knew the answer.

"And some!"

Bob`s next question for Sophie was totally unpredictable and caught her off guard.

"How many rolls of toilet paper do you use?"

"What?" Ignoring her request for clarification, Bob continued.

"She`s averaging fourteen a week - not the cheap stuff. We`re talking five quid a roll." Sophie was temporarily sympathetic towards Bob.

"What`s it made from, unicorn fur? Has she got a problem?"

"Yes! She spends too much money on bog roll." Bob`s face began to turn a deep shade of red. "It`s not even for our use!"

Sophie`s expression said it all so Bob explained.

"She uses most of it to line the cage of that stupid, posh bird of hers."

Bob started angrily sorting through the daily post that sat in a pile on the desk; Sophie, perplexed by the whole conversation said nothing for a moment, but she hated silences so thought of something to say.

"Things still not great between you two?" Distracted by the letters, Bob didn`t reply immediately, but when he did it was with an air of resignation.

"We keep muddling through." Bob`s blood pressure began to increase as did the pile of opened envelopes. "Bills! Bills! More bills! Look at them all."

Sophie suddenly remembered the start of the conversation.

"Aren't you going to sort the amp out for Mr. Johnson?"

Bob stopped calculating how much today`s tranche of invoices would cost and looked at Sophie.

"Can't you get this one; he winds me up."

"Everyone winds you up! I'm busy. You'll have to do it." She shot him a glare that basically meant - it was his job. Bob turned around and slunk off down the corridor towards studio `A`.

* * *

The studio was adequate in size with enough room to take the duo; Knobby sat behind a drum kit and Johnson sang while playing an acoustic guitar. It was a typical rehearsal studio; badly in need of redecoration to mask the faint smell of a bygone era; sweat and nicotine had built up over years of clammy musicians smoking their way through tune, after tune, after tune. Bob waited outside for a convenient moment to interrupt his paying guests; the moment didn't happen so he barged in regardless displaying his very best customer relations skills.

"What the hell is the problem this time?"

Johnson remained calm in the face of his goading, he had come to expect this level of service from Bob.

"Your equipment is faulty - And the toilet is broken." His cutting reply had a hint of sarcasm - Bob had come to expect this level of brusqueness from his clients. However, the delivery of an additional piece of bad news meant, for the moment, Johnson had the upper hand.

"What do you mean?" he asked feeling a little indignant.

"I was just sitting down playing away to myself and I smelt burning." Bob saw an opportunity to score a point.

"What the toilet caught fire?" Although delivered in a soft tone, the sentiment was razor sharp.

"No - the amp..." Clearly Johnson was vexed and this display of weakness meant Bob could mentally chalk up a point; however the advantage was short-lived when the facts were qualified. "The toilet broke when Knobby shoved the amp down it to put the flames out."

Studio facilities damaged by its own equipment failures was a huge own goal, so Johnson chalked up two points and now held the whip hand. He started to call the shots. "Sort out a replacement – quick as you can."

13

"What the amp or the toilet?" Bob bristled and attempted to throw one last, futile obstacle in the way but Johnson batted it away.

"Both. We have a gig tonight and Knobby has I.B.S."

Wounded by this skirmish, Bob shuffled out the studio leaving Johnson smirking at his band mate. Knobby, an old-school hippy at heart, really disliked confrontation which often made him wonder why they bothered using this particular studio.

* * *

Sophie appeared at the door with a fresh amplifier, obviously she had been dispatched by Bob who had run out of nice things to say.

"Here you go." She plugged the new unit in, then picked up a spare guitar and began to test the amp with a blistering solo, full of rhythm and energy that made Knobby smile. He knew talent when he heard it and as any fellow performer would, felt duty bound to join in. The jam session lasted a few minutes then came to a natural halt.

"Hey, you're pretty good." Sophie complimented Knobby. "Where do you normally play?"

"Pubs mainly." Knobby felt uneasy, he knew Sophie was a great musician and probably far more experienced than him. Packing her guitar away, she carried on talking.

"Is that mainly with Mr. J?"

"Yeh." Knobby paused in thought before continuing. "I used to jam with my sister as well."

"What does she play?" ask Sophie.

"Mainly guitar; she's a brilliant soloist, a bit like you." Sophie blushed at this tribute and being a naturally modest individual, steered the conversation away from herself.

"What other interests do you have?" Knobby contemplated his answer before replying - he had a glint of mischief in his eye.

"I'm a keen photographer."

"That sounds cool; do you do weddings?"

"No - funerals mainly." came the unexpected response.

Sophie thought she had misconstrued the slightly peculiar answer and replayed it in her head. Having enjoyed the confusion caused, Knobby continued with his outlandish claim.

"People want a record of the big day so I get them lined up outside the church; first the widow with the coffin, followed by the extended family..." He glanced quickly at Sophie to check if the fog was lifting; it wasn't so he carried on. "...then the pallbearers often want one of those quirky lads' poses; usually one of them is still hung over from the post-mortem..."

"Too much embalming fluid?" Sophie had finally synced into Knobby's wavelength and realised he also had an off-beat sense of humour.

"Exactly!" said Knobby, now knowing they were on the same page.

Sophie carried on with the comic thread.

"Don't tell me; you then capture the moment when the wreath is thrown over the widow's shoulder to see who will be next?" She beamed across the room at the drummer. "I thought you were being serious for a moment."

"Just my sense of absurd wit." He winked.

"I'm used to it, my brother has the same bizarre outlook on life. You should meet him."

"Anytime." Knobby smiled.

Sophie suddenly felt she was intruding on their valuable studio time, glancing at her watch, she made her excuses and left.

Making her way towards the back office, Sophie passed the other studios which lined the corridor - from behind closed doors, various strains of odd bits of tunes could be heard. A chorus here, a verse there, all in different keys and tempos. Stopping and listening to the cacophony she became philosophical, likening the studios to the global community, each room representing a different country producing its own rhythm of life.

"If only they all stopped for a moment and actually listened to their neighbours, they would realise the same tune is being played universally." She said out loud. "Then they could all play together... and not give me such a bloody headache."

Sophie had been suffering from random pains in the head for a couple of days now which she just put down to Bob-related stress.

* * *

The back office was a mess, but provided a small sanctuary where Sophie could go and hide to escape from everything. After shoving the door to, she sat down in front of something that once resembled a desk, stretched out her arms over a pile of papers and rested her head on them. The window was open and provided a gentle breeze, on which was carried the drone of a Radio Four announcer, delivering the shipping forecast from a distant radio. She closed her eyes and started to float away.

Time drifted onwards; Sophie slumbered but just before she managed twenty of her forty winks, she became aware of a creaking noise which seamed vaguely familiar. She woke with a start and stood bolt upright.

"The room's moving!" she said loudly, in order to convince herself it was actually happening. Sure enough the office listed to one side and the sound of creaking timbers was the same as before. Sophie looked herself up and down. Nelson was back! The breaking waves on Victory's bow and the shouts of marines once again provided the soundtrack. Revision time again! Sophie strode purposely towards the door, opened it and stepped through.

Alone in the wardroom, Sophie surveyed the situation. The sunlight flooded through the small windows, more so than before; deducing that time had moved on, she realised the battle was looming ever closer. She considered all her the options carefully, then bellowed in the direction of the quarter deck.

"Hardy, a quick word please." She figured he would be in earshot. Sure enough, as before Mr. Johnson, dressed as the officer came striding through the door and saluted.

"Yes, Sir!" he said in a Royal Navy sort of way.

"The shipping forecast says there's a storm brewing. Maybe we should contact Admiral Villeneuve to see if we can bring the start time forward; no point making things difficult for ourselves."

"Maybe we could ask him to postpone it a day or so?" He proposed an alternative option, but Sophie knew that the battle had to take place in the next couple of hours or the historical facts would be changed forever. Although she momentarily considered and relished the thought of being solely responsible for altering the course of history -on reflection she couldn't be bothered to re-sit the last two years of college just to re-learn the facts. She needed an excuse.

"I just remembered, I've left my dog in kennels."

"So?"

"Their prices are extortionate! Another couple of days out here would cost an arm and a leg..." She looked down at her empty jacket sleeve. "...which I simply can't afford. You must contact Villeneuve immediately."

"Yes, Sir!" Johnson snapped to attention. He reached for his mobile and poked at the screen only to discover the battery was dead. He looked at Sophie; she glared back at him with the same stare Bob had been administered earlier. Instinctively, Mr. J knew he had to improvise.

"Leave it with me." he said turning to exit the room.

Sophie was alone once more and pondered on what to do next.

A large, ornate writing desk which Sophie hadn't noticed before, sat in the far corner; out of curiosity, she wondered over and lifted the lid to inspect the contents. Inside there was a phone charger and an old fashioned transistor radio; she looked at the charger and had half a mind to call out to Johnson, but the radio intrigued her more. Picking it up, she turned the volume dial round until static, fuzz and hiss were audible. Then twisting the tuning control various strains of music and voices faded in and out of Sophie's scope. The shipping forecast was the first recognisable soundscape she found; it was still warning of an impending storm around the cape.

"I know this already!" Sophie informed the announcer. She continued to spin the dial, and gradually the familiar sounds of `Sweet Home Alabama` filled the airwaves. She always enjoyed a bit of country rock and began to strut around, the music compelling her to mime along with her air-guitar. The sounds of Lynyrd Skynyrd at their finest rattled around the wardroom, but were interrupted by the shouted conversation from outside. Sophie listened while continuing to mimic the rocky guitar; the British officer was the first to bellow loudly.

"Yo! Villeneuve."

There was a slight pause, then a very faint but dismissive French voice could be heard in response.

"Oui?"

"I say old chap, could we kick things off a bit earlier; say around twelve noon?"

There was another slight pause, possibly due to translation issues, possibly due to the indifference of the speaker. Eventually the French Commander replied.

"Oui, see you later."

"Great! I'll get the boss to keep an eye out for you."

The last comment made Sophie chuckle to herself, but it was a good revision point. She began to trawl through her memory banks and recite out loud.

"Although partially blinded in his right eye at Corsica in seventeen- ninety four, Nelson didn't wear a patch as he..." She stopped, dead in her tracks. Panic started to set in - Sophie had been spinning and wheeling around playing an elaborate air guitar solo...with both arms. Until now, she had remained true to Nelson's image by tucking her right arm inside her jacket, but currently she was giving Clapton a run for his money and Johnson was just about to drop the latch of the door and walk in. The metal handle fell and the hinges moaned about taking the weight, as Sophie fumbled hopelessly with the heavy felt lapels of her tunic. The door creaked open and she only just managed to thrust the offending arm into her tunic before her subordinate officer noticed anything unusual.

"All sorted, Sir!" he said cheerfully as he strolled in. Instantly he stopped and listened to the radio. With a nod of the head in time to the music, he spoke.

"Great tune - love this one."

Chapter 2

Sophie woke with a jolt and banged her knee on the underside of the desk; she was back on dry land, in a static office with no sign of the `Victory`. A piece of paper that was stuck to the side of her mouth by dribble, fell off and floated to the floor. She stood up, rubbed her knee and cocked her head to one side. Somehow she could still hear the strains of `Sweet Home Alabama` being played somewhere.

"Did I leave the radio on in my head?" she asked, shaking her top half violently to see if that made a difference - it didn't - the music played on. In a semi-trance she meandered out the office and headed down the corridor to where she thought the sounds were coming from. Reaching the door to studio `A` she stopped outside and realised the source must be Johnson and Knobby. Pressing the door gently so not to interrupt them, it slowly swung open just ajar allowing the music to swell into her space. Sure enough, the duo were jamming the same classic track that played in her dreamscape, but Sophie struggled to understand the logic.

Standing in the doorway and peering through the gap, she realised this wasn't the only thing out of place - Johnson stood singing, playing the guitar in a normal fashion, but behind him Knobby was drumming - while sitting on a toilet - totally nonchalant as if this was perfectly ordinary. While she pondered the significance of this, by accident she leant on the door and it flew open, sending her tripping into the room. The pair of musicians immediately stopped playing and saluted while snapping to attention.

"Are they taking the piss?" Sophie thought; then she froze. Something was definitely out of place - not just the toilet-seated drummer. Taking a step back into the corridor and looking down at herself, she realised she was *still* in full battle dress complete with wig and black bicorn hat - clearly Johnson and Knobby recognised her as their superior officer.

Questions began piling up in her cerebral in-tray. Why were Hardy and Scott, nineteenth century mariners, veterans of Trafalgar, practising `Sweet Home Alabama`? Why is Knobby playing while sitting on a toilet? Why are elements of reality and fantasy being so distorted...?

This was the first time that she had felt uneasy about her delusions; normally they were liberating, but now the abnormal had reached a new, different level and Sophie wasn't quite sure why...

* * *

The phone on the untidy desk rang right in Sophie's ear; she woke with a jolt and banged her knee on the underside of the desk. A piece of paper that was stuck to the side of her mouth by dribble, fell off and floated to the floor. She stood up and looked down - everything was normal, whatever normal was...she had begun to wonder. The phone continued to ring, still slightly muddled and confused she picked up and answered.

"Caramel Two studios, Good Morning." - This was a total guess, actually she had no idea what time of day it was. The conversation that followed was fairly one sided with the voice on the other end doing most of the talking. Sophie was glad of this, her brain was still rebooting and she wasn't fully concentrating. When the caller had finished, Sophie felt obliged to repeat back the salient points - more for her own benefit.

"...so, delivery will be later today; within the hour. One piano; thank you. Oh, I nearly forgot, we need a stool to go with it...Perfect. Thanks, bye." She returned the phone to its cradle and thought for a mo. Sophie had no concept of how much time had passed since events started, but the details replayed over and over in her jumbled mind; she was desperate to find some meaning among the chaos, but realising it wasn't going to be sorted quickly, reluctantly gave up and instead went to inform Bob about the forthcoming delivery.

* * *

Bob sat in reception scratching his head with a screwdriver, the broken amplifier from earlier lay in pieces, components spread all over the counter. No matter how much he scraped the tool through his scalp or squinted through one eye, the mystery remained - how more parts had been removed from the amp, than were in it in the first place? Sophie approached and immediately recognised the problem; an imbecile was attempting to tackle a tricky job, without any formal training.

Bob`s frustration spilled out - he had an intense look on his face, a cross between anger and blind panic - like an amateur surgeon entering an operating theatre after getting a parking ticket. With reluctance and an element of caution, Sophie went to talk but to her relief, just then the main phone rang.

Bob was mid keyhole surgery, tongue poking out the corner of his mouth signifying deep concentration, without looking he reached out to pick up the phone, and while being distracted by the `patient`, answered abruptly.

"Hello!" he barked down the phone.

"Hi, is that Camel Toe studios?" The voice had a raw cockney twang with a hint of forty a day. Bob stopped tinkering and braced himself.

"No." he said firmly. "This is Caramel Two studios." Bob thought this would be the end of the conversation, but the voice continued.

"Caramel Two? What sort of name is that?" Bob felt his heckles rise.

"A slightly more commercially viable name than Camel Toe." He replied through gritted teeth.

"Only just..." the response was swift. "...I thought it was one of those post-modern ironic brand identities."

"I'm sorry, who is this?"

"The plumber, you left a message about a broken khazi." Bob`s demeanour changed in an instant; he needed the facilities up and working as soon as possible, and having spoken to many trades-people so far, this guy was the only one he hadn't yet rubbed up the wrong way. He softened his approach.

"Oh yes, thank you so much for phoning back."

"No problem, Mr. Chuff."

21

"It's Marsh!" Teeth were clenched once more.

"My secretary definitely wrote down Chuff. So anyway, regarding your enquiry - I don't have any second hand toilets at the moment, we've had a bit of a run on them this month..."

"That's nice, but ..." Bob tried to get a word in, but clearly the plumber was in full flight and didn't hear him.

"...Yeh, the pre-owned, distressed look is in vogue at the moment. Would a brand new one be ok?" Normally a posed question would be followed by a gap so an answer could be given, but the sales pitch continued. "If you want me to give it that `used` look then I could ask the lads to....."

"No!" Bob had heard enough. "A completely fresh, un-soiled, perfectly formed piece of porcelain would do fine."

"Ok. I'll send Darren round later to drop it off..." Bob sighed as a massive sense of relief washed over him - the toilet was finally going to be replaced, but more importantly this conversation could now end... except the plumber hadn't quite finished.

"...I will pop round a week Monday to plumb it in." The tension in Bob's neck had been subsiding, but returned with a vengeance.

"A week Monday! Bloody hell! Can't your lad do it when he's here later?" It seemed like a reasonable question.

"God no, he's completely useless." came the blasé reply. Bob was now getting desperate.

"Please? At least this week?"

"Not a chance; I'm completely stacked." Bob's heart sank, but just as he was about to implode, the voice threw him a possible lifeline.

"Hang on, I just had a thought." Bob's ears pricked up.

"Yes?" he said expectantly.

"Whatever happened to `Caramel One` Studios?" Now resigned to getting absolutely nowhere, Bob just wanted to get off the phone.

"It's just a name. See you a week Monday."

The phone was replaced on its stand with an element of force, and the pair of pliers lying next to the amp were picked up with a certain determination; the patient was going to suffer! Sophie, having witness only one half of the conversation wasn't sure what was going on, but could tell Bob was in a mood. She had to talk to him about the piano delivery, but more importantly another conversation was long over-due...

* * *

For a while now Sophie had become frustrated with her function band and the way Bob was, or more to the point, wasn't running it. She gathered her thoughts then spoke.

"I was wondering - when are you going to find us some gigs?" she ventured. Bob put down the pliers and tensed up, he had been expecting this question for a while but decided to dance around the subject instead of facing the music.

"What do you mean?" Sophie took a moment to study his body language, then calmly spelled out the obvious.

"Well, as our band manager you should be out there hustling for work." Bob gave an innocent gaze which peeved Sophie, so she decided to add a touch of sarcasm to illustrate her point. "So far your promise of birthdays, weddings and bar mitzvahs has turned into millenniums, coronations, and moon landings."

Bob began to feel his blood pressure rise again and once more, could only find reverse gear and was currently backing up at great speed into a corner. He blurted out the first line of defence he could think of.

"You've not done badly out of me - I've got connections - only recently, I've had talks with the promoter for the Albert Hall."

Sophie suddenly had a massive feeling of guilt, she had levelled a complaint directly at Bob but all along it appeared he had been working hard behind the scenes.

"Wow! Ok, that sounds amazing. Thank you; The Royal Albert Hall!"

"Err, no. The Albert Hall pub. In Deptford. Do you know it?" Bob clarified his claim while adverting his eyes. Sophie was unimpressed.

"Yep - it closed down last week." Her answer was fired straight from the hip. She stared coldly at Bob waiting for his next contribution to the conversation, but suspecting he had nothing of substance to give. After a short pause while Bob's brain cells re-grouped, he tried again.

"I did get you on the bill at the Roundhouse, Camden."

Sophie carried on glaring at him; her reply didn't come immediately, but when it did, it was straight from the other hip.

"You *gave* us a bill for playing at the Roundhouse, Camden."

"Well, I had to recoup my expenses somehow. All the phone calls, advertising..." Sophie couldn't let that one go.

"Advertising!" She repeated the word, only louder. "ADVERTISING! - your efforts of hastily scribbling a few, badly chosen words on the back of an envelope and sticking it in the newsagent's window was at best, feeble."

"I tried my best." For the first time Bob sounded hurt. It was true, he genuinely attempted to help Sophie in all her endeavours, but their ambitions were a generation apart. However, now angry and on a roll, Sophie continued.

"I bet your idea of an advertising budget is to slip a few quid to the local tramps and asked them to amble around, spreading the word." Bob was upset, partly because he hadn't thought of that, but mostly because he had actually put some effort into promoting that particular gig.

"I think that's a bit unfair, the expenses for that gig ran into the hundreds." Sophie's steely glare penetrated deep into Bob's conscience, and although wounded, he carried on. "I thought a `pie and punk` night was a winning idea." Sophie sensed a submissive tone, but had to point out the obvious.

"We're not even a punk band - we are a function band with a slant towards `swing`."

"That shouldn't have mattered - all you had to do was turn your amps up as loud as possible, play out of tune and five times as fast. A thrash version of `Dancing Queen` would have been epic." Sophie shook her head and mumbled.

Bob suddenly lit up, he had just remembered something that would surely restore the status quo.

"Hang on, you're forgetting, I got you a gig at the Isle of Wight Festival last year." Sophie rolled her eyes upwards.

"No you didn't - you got us a gig at *a* festival on the Isle of Wight - a weekend at a farm celebrating all things to do with mushrooms and fungi."

"Oh. I thought it was..." Sophie interrupted him to continue her monologue.

"...with cooking demos from minor celebrity chefs; a fungus hurling contest." Bob went to speak, but Sophie carried on. "...and the unforgettable, Mr. Mushroom competition. I still have nightmares about the swimwear section."

"Hang on, my contact definitely told me it was..." Bob went to launch a defence, but Sophie hadn't finished - she went into sarcastic mode.

"... and, Ladies and Gentlemen, for those of you who can be bothered, please make your way through the cow pats, past the dead badger and into the next field where we have laid on some entertainment from a bunch of very awkward looking musicians that we bussed in at literally no expense." She paused, but before she could continue, Bob stepped in, moving the subject a squint to the left as a distraction.

"Outdoor gigs are good for you, plenty of fresh air, a decent size stage to play on." Regrettably he had stumbled down another cul-de-sac.

"It was a big stage." Sophie stated, "But, unfortunately constructed from bales of hay." She glared at Bob who now looked like a man on the verge of giving up – a threshold that Sophie felt obligated to help him over. "Our singer suffers really badly from hay fever - she sneezed all the way through the disco set."

"Yes, but..."

"By the time we reached 'I will survive' her face was swollen to the size of a pumpkin - she couldn't see properly, fell off the side of the stage and stood on a rake."

"A rake?" Bob said, quizzically.

Sophie inhaled deeply, then carried on.

"Yes, a rake - which flew up, broke her nose and three teeth. Heavily concussed, she then tripped over and landed in a pile of grass."

"Soft landing then." He said weakly, trying to inject a small amount of humour into the conversation. He needn't have bothered, Sophie barely realised he spoke.

"...underneath which, was a pile of pig's poo."

"Well, it's tough at the top." Bob was now throwing in any old sound-bite into the conversation, making Sophie more irate.

"You aren't kidding! A few yokels with an uneven ratio of brain cells to pints of cider mistook her for their scarecrow. It took me ages to explain to them they don't normally wear black evening dresses."

"Look! A gig's a gig isn't it? - you got paid didn't you?"

"Nope!" came the reply.

Bob slumped - he was well and truly on the ropes - a barely coherent mumble crept out from under his breath.

"I thought my contact was dealing with that."

"We spent two miserable nights camping in mid-November..."

Bob interrupted her - he'd had enough. In the last few hours studio facilities had been vandalised, he had lost a slanging match with Johnson, and spoken to a lousy plumber who thought his name was `Chuff`. It was time to assert some authority and impart some wisdom gathered from years of experience.

"Listen, you can't always get the glamorous gigs; the rough has to be taken with the smooth.... Wait a minute!" A thought had just entered his head - a real zinger that would surely adjust the equilibrium. "Did I, or did I not get you that high profile wrap party for that `TV` crowd last summer?" Bob felt really pleased with himself for dragging that one out of the archives. Sophie sighed.

"You did, and thankfully all the transvestites thoroughly appreciated the music, but..." Sophie stopped mid-sentence; she wasn't getting anywhere, but more importantly her shift had just finished. "I don't have time for this pointless conversation, and anyway I'm now officially off the clock." Bob was very relieved to hear this and he visibly relaxed. Sophie continued. "I've got a college assignment to finish and a stack of revision - I'll be in the back office if that's ok?"

She gathered some files together and sloped off down the corridor, mumbling back at Bob as she went. "By the way, the piano delivery is due soon." Bob barely heard her; he had already stuck his head back inside the amp, still labouring under the impression he could fix it.

* * *

The main front door to the studios led first into a lobby area, then into the inner reception. Bob had tried his best to furnish the foyer with trendy pictures, a second hand sofa and a plastic palm tree, all of which made Sophie cringe every time she walked into work. It was a daily reminder that Bob didn't have a clue when it came to style or finesse. As a matter of fact he didn't have a clue how to hang pictures either - the collection remained leaning up against the tatty couch covering up an iffy looking stain.

On the main door, the previous owner had installed a switch which, when triggered sounded a buzzer near the inner reception desk. The noise it emitted was like an angry wasp with a flatulence problem and constantly made Sophie jump when patrons called in. Several requests had been placed for it to be changed, but Bob knew as much about door bells as picture hanging, so alas the electrical rasping of a farting insect continued to herald the arrival of visitors.

Sophie was deep in thought about how to tackle her revision, when she heard the buzzer sound.

"Ha!" she said, "he's got to do some actual work for a change." She continued to make notes but kept half an ear out towards the reception - it was always fun to listen to a conversation between Bob and a customer. Generally it lead to chaos, confusion and ultimately conflict. Sophie still felt aggrieved by Bob's deficiencies in his management skills and hoped that karma was calling in the form of a suitably obtuse punter. The following events surpassed even Sophie's expectations.

Although the guitar amplifier he was mending wasn't very big, Bob had managed to get his right arm lost among the wiring and semi burnt-out circuit boards, and so he could see what was actually trapping his arm, his head followed closely behind, leaving him oblivious to the visitor's presence.

The caller mooched through the reception and stood on the opposite side of the counter awaiting Bob's attention, but he remained ensconced in his work. To attract attention, the gentleman gave a little cough which startled Bob - he rapidly stood up from his hunched position and thumped his head on the way. Rubbing the sore patch vigorously in place of shouting profanities he addressed the gentleman.

"Sorry Sir - didn't see you there." Being from a certain British generation he apologised for clonking his own bonce. He then tried to explain his predicament. "Too busy fixing this amp...It got thrown into a toilet..."

The caller remained quiet, emotionless and continued to fix his gaze on Bob causing him to become very nervous. The visitor wasn't particularly intimidating, in fact he looked like a regular person; fifty-something, a little beige around the edges, but his lack of communication was beginning to faze the frustrated owner, so Bob tried a different tack.

"Did you want to hire a rehearsal room? One moment..." With his unimpeded hand, Bob began to stretch across his body almost tying himself in a knot, but despite best efforts, the keyboard of the office computer simply was out of reach. Struggling a little more and shifting his weight onto the other foot, with one last, over-extended stretch Bob's trapped arm dragged the broken amp to the brink of falling, while his free arm missed its target and knocked over a cold cup of coffee.

"No."

At last the stranger had spoken, albeit after watching Bob nearly break both elbows. Although annoyed by this, Bob thought he should ask another question.

"Maybe a set of guitar strings?" He had already swung his soggy, coffee-stained arm around in the other direction, but again was hampered by the amp acting like an anchor. The rack of accessories behind him was also positioned just out of range. The stranger spoke again.

"No. Thanks."

Bob stared back at him expecting some reaction - he smiled - it was a gentle smile, totally placid. This made Bob mad.

"Look, I'm very, very busy; I have a delivery due any moment."

There was a pause, as Bob thought for a split second that `Mr. Strange' was actually going to say something, but apart from a little cough nothing of any substance was uttered, so he ramped up the sarcasm.

"Traditionally at this point of a normal conversation, one of the parties involved would proffer further details in order to prevent the exchange of dialogue from stalling and leaving two idiots just staring at each other." Bob left a gap to check if `Strange` wanted to join in -nothing – so he continued. "Seeing as I have bugger-all left to say, it's over to you."

By this juncture, Sophie`s curiosity had got the better of her; although the stranger had been monosyllabic, from what little conversation he had, the voice sounded familiar. She wanted to peak down the corridor but without the boss seeing her - she had no intention of coming to his aid. Quietly, Sophie slid through the office door and took just enough steps so she could take a peek at Bob`s nemesis standing by the counter. Expecting to see a familiar face, the sight that met her was that of a total stranger.

"That's odd." she mumbled. "I know that voice; I swear I would have recognised him."

Just then the buzzer sounded again and Sophie's attention was drawn to the inner reception door. Through the built in window she could see a spotty teenager trying to enter the main door, while fighting with a toilet and cistern - so far, the inanimate objects were winning. She shot a glance back towards the counter, Bob had just moved and was now in full view so Sophie quickly took a step back to be outside his line of vision. She leant against the wall, chuckled to herself and predicted that a massive debacle was about to unfold - and she had a ringside seat.

"Saved by the bell!" Bob announced with healthy dollop of sarcasm. He shouted through to the main lobby area to make contact with whoever was out there.

"Afternoon!" In his mind, anyone would be better to talk to than the twit currently stood in front of him.

"Got a delivery for you." The teenager shouted back – he was only half way through the main front door and had the noise of the traffic to contend with, which wasn't going to help with communication.

Bob was relieved, having to deal with the chap outside was a perfect reason to get away from Mr. Strange. He began to excuse himself.

"I'm so sorry, my piano has arrived, and...'

"I'm stuck!" The gentleman now decided to start a conversation.

"Sorry. What?" Bob couldn't comprehend his rationale - having said nothing of any substance until now, he comes up with that. The odd-ball repeated himself.

"I said; I'm stuck."

Down the corridor, Sophie was now biting her top lip trying to suppress her giggles. She could see that the piano was in fact a toilet being delivered by a clumsy adolescent, and furthermore Mr Strange was about to amble down another conversational dead-end, taking the studio's increasingly frustrated owner with him.

"You're stuck!" Bob was now hovering between being mildly livid and downright irate. "At least you haven't got your arm wedged in a guitar amp, trying to hold a conversation with a plank of wood."

Strange remained docile and handed him a scruffy piece of paper.

"I'm looking for this address." he said. Instinctively Bob took the paper but immediately regretted it as this now obliged him to help the chap out. He stared at the scrawls in an attempt to make sense of them, but his concentration was broken by an update yelled from the depths of the front lobby.

"It's a bit awkward, mate - where do you want it?" Bob was deep in thought and didn't register the question; he was too wrapped up with the cryptic message from Strange.

"Is that a `t` or a `p`?" he asked, pointing to an illegible smudge, meanwhile the custodian of the khazi persisted with his enquiry.

"Anywhere, mate?" he shouted.

Bob was now struggling to compute all the demands on his brain; the unidentified address, the demeanour of the mystery caller, the logistics of the pending delivery. He needed to buy some time, so with a suggestion of panic, he threw a couple of random questions into the lobby.

"Have you got the right one? What colour is it?"

30

"White." came the reply.

"Nice! Just like Elton John's." There was a slight pause.

"I wouldn't know to be frank." said the confused teen.

"It's a `p`." Mr Strange finally cut in with his delayed answer bringing Bob`s attention quickly back to the problem in his immediately vicinity.

"Right, so, twenty seven, Ship Street?" Bob said, clarifying his fresh understanding of the information.

"No! Forty two, Ship Street." Strange blurted out - his reply was passive-aggressive and forced Bob to re-examine the paper.

"How the hell can that be a four and a two?" The question was never answered - once again, Bob`s attention was drawn to the inhabitant of the lobby.

"Oy! I'm parked on double yellows. Where do you want this?"

Sophie was now bursting with bottled up laughter as she witnessed Bob floundering his way through the situation. The conversation with Strange was placed on hold while Bob responded to the deliveryman.

"It's got to go into the live room - through here, second on the left." The confused teen look down at the toilet, scratched his groin and responded.

"Really?"

Bob didn't hear the doubtful tone from outside, he had already turned his attention back to Strange.

"Do you know the main roundabout at the end of the high street?"

"No." Strange was back to his one word answers.

"Ok. Do you know Canal Street?" Bob paused.

"No."

A disconnected thought suddenly struck Bob; the previous piano had been faulty and he didn't want another dodgy instrument, so he shouted through to the lobby.

"By the way, are you able to check it over? The last one had a duff lid - in fact, I want to have a little tinkle on it myself before you leave."

Sophie was now bent double trying to supress her laughter, while mascara tinted tears stained her cheeks. As she struggled to maintain some decorum, unwittingly and unwisely Bob began to feel he was gaining some control of the situation; having concluded with the delivery guy he turned back to Strange who now had a pen and note pad and was ready to receive more instructions.

"So, you go out of here, turn left, drive past a parade of shops..."

"I don't have a car." Strange interrupted Bob.

"What?"

"I don't trust vehicles with four wheels, ever since `that` accident." For a point of clarification, it was significantly vague, but Bob felt that he may have touched upon a sensitive subject and thought he had better try to be a little understanding.

"I'm so sorry. What accident?" He asked, immediately regretting doing so.

"You know that old picture called `The Hay-wain`?" Bob gave a non-committal nod - Strange carried on. "My great, great, Granddad was the bloke driving that wagon. He lost it on a corner and ended up stacking it in a river." Bob started to lose the will.

"Why am I having this conversation?" he muttered as the random drivel continued.

"... and when a Constable finally arrived, all he did was stand there and paint a picture of them. Bleeding rubber-necker! I always go everywhere by bike."

Bob couldn't gauge if he was serious or having a joke, either way all the wrong buttons were being pressed. He tried to steer the conversation back to the point.

"OK. Out of here, turn left - *pedal* past a parade of shops..."

Mr. Strange was now taking notes, albeit in a very laboured and frustrating way.

"S—h—o—p—s ..." He stretched each syllable to its breaking point and deliberated over every letter as he wrote on the pad. This was the last, but one straw – Again, Bob`s blood pressure rose and through clenched teeth, he continued.

"Then you get to a bank, and..."Strange interjected so he could take proper note.

"B-a-....n-............k....."

Sophie clutched her stomach as it was beginning to hurt through supressed laughter; seeing this guy cause her boss so much frustration with so little effort made it worthwhile being at work that day. By now, Bob`s knuckles had turned white and small, bullet like specs of spit were being catapulted out of the side of his mouth with every word.

"At the bank; Stop - go inside. Withdraw some money and GO AND BUY A BLOODY SAT-NAV!" He was now super-irritated; Mr. Strange on the other hand looked very indignant and slightly hurt that someone would talk to him in this way - it was a simple, straight forward question after all.

Bob had given up trying to communicate with the eccentric individual before him and was in desperate need of another channel to re-assert his flagging authority. Brimming with frustration he turned his attention to the delivery boy who was now trying to open the inner door with his buttocks. He was an easy target, and as the unsuspecting lad stepped backwards through the door, dragging the toilet behind him he was met by a verbal salvo, delivered with unnecessary malice.

"I bloody hope you`ve bought a stool to go with that!"

As Bob spoke these words, the lavatory was hauled through the door by the overburdened teen and dumped on the carpet, right in front of where he stood. Now realising his demand was somewhat inappropriate, Bob`s face, shoulders and social-grace, plummeted to depths as yet uncharted. The plumber`s mate would ordinarily be pleased with a successful conveyance of a convenience, but with Bob`s last words to him still ringing in his ears, he just glared at the ground looking suitably embarrassed. Strange tutted loudly, gave Bob a disproving look and spoke.

"This isn't brain surgery, y`know." He snatched the piece of paper from Bob and turned to the spotty teen. "Do you know where this is?" Clearly he had more confidence in him than Bob. Taking the slip and reading the scribbles, the adolescent was more than ready to make an exit and gestured to Strange to follow him outside. Bob was left with his head in his hands, reflecting on every innuendo of the previous conversation. Grimacing with every recollection, he slumped down on the counter-top feeling dejected.

Sophie made her way back to the office, in the first instance to apply some fresh makeup, but ultimately to continue with her revision. The preceding farce had been a great distraction, however she now needed to knuckle down with her studies.

* * *

The door buzzer sounded again. Bob twitched nervously, deliberating if `Captain Chaos and the Khazi Kid` were coming back for round two - he really couldn't face another tête-à-tête like the one he had just endured. The door opened, Johnson walked in closely followed by Knobby – Bob`s heart sunk. Johnson strode up to the counter and spoke first.

"I see the new toilet has arrived. Probably a good idea to install it in the restroom, rather than the hall-way."

"Really? I was going to put it your studio, thought it would complement your guitar playing." Bob left a pause; not enough so Johnson could react, but sufficient for the insult to hit its mark. He continued. "If you could attempt not to trash this one, I would be grateful."

"If you could provide us with some non-flammable equipment, I would be grateful." Johnson parried Bob`s comment with an equally infantile reply. After months of petty skirmishes, both parties had mastered the art of superficial politeness which disguised an undercurrent of full blown contempt. The trouble was, the rationale behind this mutual disdain was long lost on the pair; it was now just a default setting.

"A set of strings...P-l-ease." Johnson said finally breaking the awkward silence. Bob had somehow managed to free himself from the confines of the amp and reaching behind him made his selection - the dustiest, scruffiest looking packet he could find. Half throwing, half passing them in Johnson`s vague direction, he spoke through a phoney smile.

"Five quid...P-l-ease." Johnson selected the most dog-eared, grubbiest looking fiver and threw it directly at Bob, then gathered the strings along with his wallet and went to leave. Bob hadn't quite finished with him yet.

"I hear the landlord complained about your performance last night." Knobby could see where this was going; they had been here many times before and he wanted to defuse the situation. This would require the same level of diplomatic skills normally employed by `U.N` envoys – regrettably the closest Knobby had been to the New York based, United Nations building was Swansea.

"I blame the bar staff - I reckon they must have been putting the punters off." said Knobby. "The lot in the other bar were better, that side was heaving."

"There were also loads of people stood outside - all non-smokers" replied Bob, adding a subtle punch-line.

"I noticed that!" Knobby was enthusiastic and had an air of innocence around him, which sometimes went against him. "At least we sounded good."

"I thought we had a great set." Mr. J. interjected.

"He mentioned your set did grate." Came the snide comment from Bob. Twisting Johnson`s own words against him scored double points. He glared at Bob, assessing what sort of response he should give.

"You're being very vaginistic today - more so than normal." While Bob was occupied determining the definition of this new word, he continued. "The misses still spending all the profits?"

Johnson had successfully cancelled out Bob`s double point score with two, well executed verbal uppercuts. The studio owner needed to turn the conversation around.

"Talking of money - the hourly room rate has gone up."

"W-what? Wait, when?"

And so, with one simple sentence Johnson was on the back foot again; Bob knew it and went for the knockout.

"Immediately! I'm due a delivery of the wife's toilet paper any day."

"What?" Johnson was confused and exasperated in equal measure.

"I also have a new guitar amp and toilet to pay for." Bob was on a roll.

The pair started to bicker like a couple of pre-teen siblings, but with less rationality.

"You can't do that; we block booked."

"I can, and I have."

"I refuse to pay any extra money!"

"Then you will be hearing from my solicitor."

"I could bleeding murder you sometimes."

"Then you will be hearing from my coroner. Come on pay up."

By now, Bob was so full of rage his judgement had become clouded and all social filters suspended. He saw Johnson was still clutching his wallet and just to make a point rather than actually mug him, lunged at the poor customer grabbing his hand and started to prise his fingers open. In an instant the pair were locked in a battle of strength.

Sophie had been vaguely aware that an altercation was taking place, but being down the corridor and her mind deep in thought about Nelson`s fate, hadn't fully realised the extent that it had escalated to. Bizarrely, it was the lack of raised voices that drew her attention. She leapt out the chair and sprinted down the corridor to find out why the shouting had stopped; the sight which greeted her was one that even she thought she would never see.

Bob and Johnson were rolling around on the floor in a knot, while Knobby was stood over them. He was trying to release the grip of whoever`s hand was sticking out of the revolving mass every time they came round full circle. Sophie had seen enough.

"STOP THIS!" she yelled at the top of her voice. It had no effect, so marching over to the writhing mass on the floor, Sophie bent over to intervene, but at the same time Knobby saw an opportunity to grab at a couple of limbs as they were thrust out of the carnage - he didn't know who they belonged to and he didn't care. Grabbing the two wrists he nearly managed to force them apart. Then it happened.

The strength of the two fighters suddenly over-powered Knobby and his errant fist went flying upwards, striking Sophie, broadside across her head. She stumbled, fell backwards and lay in a heap. Still.

The three chaps stopped and stared in disbelief at what had just happened; no one wanted this. Sophie was the one person whom each of them genuinely held in high regard, but now she was incapacitated due to their actions. It would have been very easy for them to start a slanging match to lay blame in one direction or another, but mutually they knew it wasn't the time for arguing. Bob spoke first.

"Soph! Sophie!" She didn't move. "Oh my Lord. Can you hear me?"

* * *

A few moments passed before Sophie stirred, she was in pain, but at first couldn't work out why. Slowly, sensations started to return and she realised someone was propping her up to offer some comfort as she lay, half on the floor and half on Bob. He spoke again.

"My Lord. Can you hear me?" She went to answer him, but stopped before any words formed. The floor moved in a familiar, rocking sensation accompanied by a rhythmical creaking sound just as before. The light was very dim, which she put down to only having her eyes partially open, but despite this she could tell she wasn't in the studio any more. Sophie struggled but eventually managed to open her eyes wider to take in more details. She looked down. Her apparel was again, full navy regalia and logically she deduced, the poor lighting was due to being located in the bowels of HMS Victory. Sophie was weak, but managed to adjust her glance to either side; she was surrounded by her commanding officers. And Bob.

Her mind tripped over itself trying to work out what the hell was going on. Obviously the events of the Battle of Trafalgar were reaching their conclusion; this was the death of Nelson.

Sophie felt groggy herself, but clearly hadn't been shot through the shoulder like the great man himself. So what was wrong? The familiar faces of Johnson, Knobby and Bob came into view and, just like before had taken on the appearance of their characters from Nelson's navy. She gathered her wits and spoke.

"Hardy, old friend."

"Yes, my Lord?" he responded.

"What news of the battle?" She guessed Nelson would have asked that question as he lay mortally wounded on the boards of the orlop deck.

"Sir, we have routed the enemy. This victory will go down in history as one of the most famous sea battles ever fought."

Sophie began to feel slightly odd; she coughed, a deep cough and writhed in discomfort. She looked upwards through misty eyes.

"Kiss me, Hardy."

"Kiss your, what?"

Sophie ignored him - the situation was becoming very distressing. Although she knew this was a dream, she did actually feel a degree of discomfort and this confused and concerned her.

"Am I injured badly?"

"You were punched in the face by a drummer." came the reply. Nothing made sense anymore; her dreamscapes were supposed to be a domain over which she had total control, but now Sophie lay in the heat of battle, somehow injured; perhaps dying?

"Maybe if I snap out of this fantasy, everything would be ok?" she said to herself. Sophie racked her brains to come up with a point of reference - something that wasn't around at the time which, if mentioned could wake her from this dreamland. Finally she spoke to Johnson with a frail voice.

"Should I not make it old friend, I ask of two things. Please don't let them bury me at sea."

"Of course My Lord. And the second thing?"

"That statue of me in London. Ask them why it's so bloody tall - no one can actually see my face."

Sophie thought she had done enough, but as she lay there, contemplating if it had worked, she coughed. And again. And again. Something wasn't right.

"Why am I not sitting at the reception desk, arguing with Bob about some trivial matter?" she thought. Sophie truly didn't feel well but couldn't give herself a reasonable explanation as to why. Continuing to splutter, she looked up.

"I feel weak...I'm going ...."

Bob leant forward to whisper something, she could feel his breath on her cheek. As he spoke, she closed her eyes.

"Sir, before you go - did you know, if you've have had an accident at work that wasn't your fault, you can make a claim? Here are some forms." He thrust some papers at Sophie, but they just fell to the deck.

"I'm still waiting on the pay-outs for the eye and arm." she said from behind closed eyes. Sophie began to feel weaker, and her breathing was now laboured; although her mind was still ticking over, she began to relax as a feeling of serenity had begun to descend. Reaching out towards Bob she clenched his hand and spoke.

"It's too late." She exhaled slowly, relaxed, and her body slumped.

* * *

Chapter 3

A female vicar shuffled through the congregation and made her way towards the pulpit, passing a coffin which was set front and centre. A union flag was draped over the casket and a pair of ceremonial swords lay crossed at one end. Reaching the top of the stairs, she paused to look across the vast gathering that had filled St Pauls - the responsibility of leading a state funeral was making her nervous. Taking her position at the lectern and grabbing both edges of the desk in order to steel herself, she took a deep breath, looked up and spoke.

"Lords, Ladies and Gentlemen. We are gathered here today to pay our last respects to Vice Admiral, Horatio Nelson: First Viscount and First Duke of Bronte, KB. - Or `Sophie` as he was affectionately known. A man of vision, well fifty percent vision; a man of great courage - in the heat of battle he stood shoulder to shoulder with rank and file men, bearing arms ...one arm, in the face of the enemy."

She paused for dramatic effect and was about to continue when she became aware of an electronic `beeping` sound; the rhythm was slow but regular, like a dripping tap. She looked around but couldn't immediately find the source. Trying her best to ignore the interruption, the eulogy continued.

"He always knew how to rally the men; always how to pick the right words at the right time, to instil confidence and trust in his leadership. Having served under his command during the battle at Copenhagen, I will never forget... his words... to me, as we ... were moments... away.... from engaging.... the... enemy for the...... first... time."

The vicar stopped; her last sentence had become very disjointed as the beeping sound became more prominent. Instinctively she was staggering her phrasing to try to weave the words of tribute into the silent gaps. Frustrated

by this interruption, she glanced up from her notes an
identify what the foreign sound was.

She stared out into the expanse of the cathedral; the cu
disappeared. The coffin had gone. She was alone.

* * *

Sophie lay on the bed; still. It somehow felt different from normal but couldn't work out why.

Slowly, she became aware that all her movements were constricted - she tried to move her legs; nothing happened - her head wouldn't lift off the pillow. Fearing the worst she starting asking questions.

"Am I tied down?" Sophie always thought herself a level headed person, but she had to fight hard to stop herself from becoming anxious.

"Think! I don't feel anything around my legs or arms, so I can't be restrained." She lay there thinking of a million things all at once, but came to no conclusion to any of the conundrums. The rhythmical beep continued to echo through her mind - momentarily it transported her back to the early days of piano lessons - the teacher would set a metronome to beat a regular tempo for her to practice with; this new beat now marked the passage of time, but for different reasons.

She calmed down a little and considered all the facts; the noise had actually been in her head for a couple of days now, a constant background accompaniment to her thoughts and dreams; day and night, keeping her awake...

Sophie became aware of the door opening - the very same door which she had gone through moments earlier...wasn't it? Her thoughts were now, truly disorientated. A voice spoke which again sounded through her internal PA system; the same calming and familiar voice as before, only this time it was addressing someone else.

"Good morning, Doctor." said Sophie's mum.

"I'm in hospital! What am I doing in hospital?" The enormity of the situation hit Sophie like a freight train, panicking she tried talking to ask her mum

as going on. Nothing happened. She endeavoured to reach out to grab
rm. Nothing happened. Desperate to rise up and throw a hug around
, she attempted to move but nothing happened. Another, familiar voice
ke, as it did Sophie's mind raced to identify it.

"Hi, how are you today?" Images of faces flickered in and out of her mind's
ye at an alarming rate, suddenly one popped up which fitted the voice, and
Sophie was taken aback by who it was. The strange visitor to the studios who
had made her laugh so much by giving Bob a hard time - he was her
consultant! Truly, nothing made any sense.

"I'm OK. Coping - just about." Sophie's mum paused to compose herself
and keep her emotions in check. "I've been talking to her about all sorts of
things like you suggested. She can hear me, right?"

"That's a very complex question, but the short answer is yes, I believe she
can..." Sophie's mum suddenly had doubt in her mind and needed
reassuring.

"But, she's in a coma..."

And there it was. All of Sophie's questions answered in five simple words.

"But Mum, I'm fine!" Sophie yelled out at the top of her voice inside her
head. Mum didn't react. Sophie tried again. "Mum, I'm all good!" Still nothing.

Sophie was now so desperate to communicate with her mum she was
shouting, kicking and screaming inside in an attempt to attract attention, but
she neither moved nor made a sound. Emotions started to course through her
mind and at this point the prevailing one was frustration; she just wanted to
tell her mum all was well. In fact, in her mind she had never felt better.

Sophie lay and thought of the implications of what had just transpired; a
major piece of her life's jigsaw had fallen out of reach, but at least it explained
why her imagination had become more surreal and detached from reality than
usual. Doctor Strange spoke again to try and calm her mum's fears.

"The brain is an amazing organ, anything you can do to stimulate her
thought processes will help. Any details from Sophie's past could trigger
something - big or small." Mum nodded, as the doctor continued. "Music can
be good. What sort does she like?"

"All types. She played in a few bands. I've got some recordings of her somewhere at home."

"You should bring them in, music has a great power over our emotions." Her mum paused to compose herself before speaking again.

"She looks peaceful just lying there. I like to think of her as just resting; nothing more." Doctor Strange gave a kindly smile and nodded.

"What have you got there?"

"Old college notes from the history course she was doing - I've been reading them to her."

"Sounds like a good idea. What was the topic?" Sophie's mum picked up a folder and opened it to the cover page and read the title.

"The Battle of Trafalgar. Twenty-first October, Eighteen-o-five."

Mum looked up from the bedside and addressed the doctor.

"You do think I'm getting through?"

"Yes. I'm absolutely positive you are." said the doctor.

Chapter 4

Sophie lay on the bed, still confused about what had transpired. In her mind she wasn't lying in hospital attached to a life-support machine, but could get up and move around at will. In better times her mind would soar and wheel around like a bird on the wing, darting from one thought to another without hindrance from logic or reason and it was this that helped refuel her soul with positivity and optimism. She was fortunate not to have lost this attribute in her current predicament; if anything it had been heightened.

* * *

An hour had gone by since Sophie's mum left - she had whispered a goodnight to her sleeping daughter and on the way out, gently kissed her forehead. Fully aware of this, Sophie had a little wobble at this point - not because she was afraid of being alone, more that she wanted to afford mum some peace of mind but didn't know how. Subdued thoughts filtered through her mind, summing up the situation.

"The only channel of communication I have with the outside world - the only thing that is reminding folks that I'm still here, is that bloody machine that goes `beep` every time my heart beats."

Her internal voice began to tense up showing signs of frustration - she instinctively knew this was not the correct path to take – it led to a dark side - a route that she had no intention of taking. To move away from this corrosive emotion, thoughts about her mum and their relationship quickly filled Sophie's mind. She had always been a calming influence in her life – it was like having a best friend who also offered guidance across her formative years and beyond. As she reminisced, mum's voice echoed throughout Sophie's head, repeating the most valuable and appropriate slice of wisdom she had imparted... "Always react to any circumstance with a positive and measured response." It was short and concise, but fitted her current quandary perfectly. Bolstered by mum's stoic philosophy, Sophie's confidence was rejuvenated.

"Come on Soph. You can do this." She started to give herself a pep talk. "Where's your stiff upper lip?" Adopting a more formal tone to her voice, the motivational speech continued. "Just remember; you're British! You know; the old bull-dog spirit." For some reason her voice had now taken on a slightly deeper, very plummy 'RAF' quality. She chuckled to herself and continued. "This is Nighthawk calling Danny Boy; do you read me?"

She loved all genres of movies, but especially the old war films where the commanding officers were straight out of Eton and the cockney, lower ranks dropped more H's than bombs. The college course Sophie had been taking covered the 'thirty-nine to 'forty-five conflict a few terms ago, and being comparatively recent history it was a period that she could relate to. Artefacts from the time could be handled, places directly involved visited, and - most pertinently - people who lived through it could impart first-hand experiences. Pages from her reference books would come to life when a veteran passed comment... "Oh yes, I remember that happening...it was a bright summers evening in 'forty-four..." Her appreciation of the text went to a whole new level.

It was this ability to almost reach out and touch history that Sophie revelled in, not in a sensationalist way - she would just be in awe of how people managed to get through whatever situation they found themselves in, no matter how dark and terrifying. Subconsciously, she was applying this same bravado to her predicament.

She settled down and started to play around with her new voice.

"What-O; I see Jerry has advanced again." Sophie chuckled before thinking up another cliché. "I say, Squiffy old bean, you couldn't pour me another livener could you?"

Suddenly, her concentration was broken by a very unusual sound for a hospital corridor. Weighty footsteps that could have only been made by a troupe of heavy duty boots marching in unison, took Sophie by surprise. She sat bolt upright and adjusted her head in order to eavesdrop more efficiently. As the footsteps began to fade, they came to a dramatic stop with a double time `stomp`. Then... silence.

"Blimey, these hospital porters are well drilled these days." Sophie mused, but her thoughts were soon interrupted when voices struck up a conversation. Although muffled, if she listened closely the odd word could be picked out.

"They`re talking in German!"

Then she heard something that made her curiosity peak.

"Willkommen bei Stalag Luft." There was a pause, then an emphatic instruction was delivered in *very* plain English.

"Don't try to escape. It is futile."

Sophie slid off the bed and made her way towards the door, passing the old, heavy-framed mirror that hung on the wall. She stopped and stared at the reflection.

"I don't remember growing a moustache; certainly not one as bushy as this." She stroked the facial hair with a mixture of pride and bewilderment. Then, noticing the uniform, her new persona was complete; full RAF fatigues, emblazoned with `Wing Commander` stripes on both sleeves. Looking towards the door, she hesitated.

"Ok, I've got nothing in the diary for today; let`s go and see what this is about."

She straightened her shoulders, spun round on the heels of impeccably polished shoes and instinctively marched towards the exit, arms alternately swinging in opposition to her legs. Upon reaching the door without hesitation she opened it and peered out.

* * *

The freezing night air instantly stole Sophie`s breath as she stepped through the door. Light from the full moon bounced off snow clad surfaces and illuminated the scene of row upon row of wooden huts, all raised up on legs. To her left there was a large exercise area with a small allotment running along the south side and to her right sat a *very* small hut enclosed by its own razor wire border. All around the perimeter was a tall fence that extended beyond sight; clearly it was designed as a demarcation line between freedom and captivity - its perfect line only interrupted by imposing watch towers set at regular intervals.

An eerie silence shrouded the area and apart from the odd, thin wisp of smoke emanating from improvised chimneys, the cabins appeared to be lifeless. Except one. Sited across a narrow gangway opposite Sophie was a hut with a dim light flickering from behind an improvised curtain. She stared at the window and after her eyes had adjusted to the ambient light, Sophie could make out a faint silhouette moving around inside.

Just for a moment, Sophie deliberated if she should return to her bed and the reassurance of the machine that beeped, or take a step into the unknown. With comparatively nothing to lose, Sophie smiled; another trip to the past was a great reason to go forward and uncannily, she had a reassuring feeling about the occupant of the cabin. Instinctively she looked both ways to ensure the coast was clear and hurried across the compound towards hut `104`.

Reaching the steps that lead to the door, she suddenly became aware of approaching footsteps from within the darkness between two huts. Clearly this was just another coma induced dreamscape, but until she got her bearings Sophie decided that it wouldn't be good to be caught outside after lockdown. She leapt up the wooden stairs and tried the latch - it was stiff but on the second attempt and with a nudge of her shoulder, the door released and she charged in. Quickly resetting the handle, Sophie immediately went to the window and peered through a rip in the makeshift blind. A German sentry taking his Alsatian for a walk had sauntered into view; he stopped to light a cigarette while the dog peed up the side of the hut; then they moved on. She was safe.

The hut was split into two sections; the sleeping quarters had very little in it apart from some rustic looking bunk-beds, and the other half only had a small stove sited in the corner and a basic table with two chairs.

"Haven't these guys heard of Ikea?" she muttered.

"There you are, Sir; bit parky out there?" Sophie jumped.

A tall figure emerged from the gloom of the sleeping quarters - she stood and stared. It was Johnson, again he was making an impromptu appearance in her dream.

"Game of cards, WingCo?" he said producing a deck from his breast pocket. Sophie's imagination was fired up once more; Johnson was dressed in full squadron leader regalia and also spoke with a public school drawl. Sophie's mind raced to gather her thoughts together; at least the Nelson jaunt to Trafalgar was made with a clear head - albeit while comatose - but this was different. She sat down at the table where Johnson was already shuffling the pack. He looked at her and spoke.

"So... you were saying?" Sophie froze; surely they had only just met?

"Sorry?"

"Just before you popped outside, you were telling me about your last raid." Sophie's mind started to trawl through her college notes, but for some reason the only results found were fragments of information which made no sense. Then, she had a moment of inspiration - having watched countless old movies, all she had to do was weave their significant plot points into an articulate account of events. The concept was solid, but she lacked preparation.

"There I was, flying through the night sky; Red leader had taken a tumble and the rest of my squadron were nowhere to be seen. The fuel gauge was shot - didn't have a clue how much juice I had. Suddenly, the mighty Imperial fortress came into sight..." She took a moment to look at Johnson - he was hanging off every word like an excitable child, eyes wide open with anticipation and a big smile on his face.

"Wow! What did it look like?" he interjected, enthusiastically.

Without really giving it any thought, Sophie continued.

"What the Death Star? Big. Round. Grey...enough fire power to destroy a small planet..." She stalled; the last sentence didn't sound quite right. Looking at Johnson again she expected him to be scratching his head, instead he eagerly fired off another question.

"How the bally-heck did you manage that all on your own?"

Sophie decided to keep going; she was as keen to see how this story ended as much as Johnson.

"Well, I was just about to make an approach, when I noticed one of our lads coming in from the west...."

"How could you tell it was one of ours?" interrupted Johnson.

"What, the Millennium Falcon? I would recognise that craft anywhere." She began to relax and go with the flow.

"Wow! The Falcon!" Johnson was now on the edge of his seat and bouncing with excitement - he wanted every detail.

"Who was piloting?"

"That Dutch lad, Han."

"Solo?"

"No, he had a co-pilot with him. Really hairy fellow..."

"Chewbacca?"

"No. Clive somebody."

Clearly Sophie's brain had some crossed wires, however the quirky exchange was somewhat enjoyable so she carried on.

"Our spies had identified a weakness in their defence; the central trench lead directly to an internal ammo dump."

"My word, Sir - it must have been very well defended?"

"It was. Their guns opened up and my R2 unit took a direct hit."

"They took your radar out!" Johnson took a sharp intake of breath.

"Yup! Bally bad luck really. My steering flange had taken a bucket of shells; basically I had no way of controlling the plane and operate the forward guns at the same time."

Johnson had put his cards down and was now tapping out his pipe on the edge of the table.

"Hmm, sticky wicket - what did you do?"

Sophie needed some thinking time, the storyline had become a little fuzzy and somewhat removed from her original brief.

"Well, a strange thing happened...." Leaving that sentence hanging to add to the drama, she picked up the cards Johnson had dealt her and slowly sorted them into suits. Eventually, having played out the scene in her head, she leant towards Johnson, softened her voice to add tension and continued.

"...I kept hearing the ghostly voice of an old music- hall actor."

"Really, what did he say?" Johnson was bemused.

"Use the fork."

"That's bizarre." He was mystified by this, but also intrigued by this revelation.

"Totally bizarre." agreed Sophie. She continued. "Then I remembered, I had pinched some cutlery from the mess hall just before the balloon went up..."

Johnson's face lit up as he suddenly pieced together how his WingCo was able to escape from this tight squeeze. Tripping over his own words he proudly predicted the end to Sophie's story.

"Let me guess, you jammed the fork in the steering flange to steady the craft leaving you hands-free to let loose with the front rattlers." Sophie was grateful to Johnson for completing the tale.

"Bingo! I radioed The Falcon and said, let's blow this thing and go home."

"Bravo, Sir! Another, truly remarkable story to tell the grandkids?"

"One of many... too many - I wouldn't know where to begin." she said heroically.

"You could start with the fourth one, Sir." he added with a glint of mischief in his eye.

This contemporary quip from Johnson was enough to make Sophie snap-to - she became aware that, rather than wasting time mixing up her movies, she should try to find out the fate of her fellow imprisoned airmen - more importantly her own destiny. Looking down at the random selection of cards, she stared at them studying her options. The black and red symbols started to blur into one another as the different layers of her mind began to work at separate speeds; the upper most, superficial strata worked on which card to lead with, the subterranean level wanted to dig deep to find meaning, maybe even a correlation between her fantasies and reality. Then a revelation struck.

Her imagination had created an allegory to illustrate the situation; the coma was trapping her mind within her own body - the P.O.W camp physically confined Sophie within her own mind. Now, she had to play the hand that life had dealt her.

The concept felt alien at first, but as Sophie mulled it over, some perspective on where she was, not physically but mentally, was proffered. She quickly drew a comparison between her two worlds.

"Maybe if I could escape from this prison camp, I would also be released from my coma?" she positively concluded. This thought filled her with a sense of optimism as she had a degree of control over the events in her fantasy world. Now refocused she looked at Johnson, slammed the cards down on the table and returned to her alter-ego; standing up to assert more authority, she took the initiative.

"Priority number one, Squadron Leader; we need to get out of here. We must get the tunnels finished."

"Yes Sir!"

"We need to speed up the excavation processes; the camp commandant is getting twitchy - we need more diversions."

Johnson slumped down in his chair in a slightly unorthodox manner and casually crossed his legs up on the table.

"Not more diversions! The traffic is murder at rush hour as it is..." He responded nonchalantly, but this was not the reaction Sophie was expecting.

"Pardon?" she said, confused as to why Johnson`s demeanour had dramatically changed. He ignored her and continued.

"How long does it take to dig up a road, anyway?"

"Excuse me, Squadron Leader. What are you talking about?"

Confusion started to spread throughout Sophie`s thoughts as her mind became fuzzy; disorientated she sat down clasping her hands around her head to help steady her equilibrium. Senses were suddenly being overloaded as sight and sounds became acutely amplified causing her to become very distressed; it was as if her brain had become detuned resulting in static interference on all channels. She moved her hands down to protect her ears from the onslaught and clamped both eyes shut to stop them from being overburdened. The background noise in her head started to crescendo to an unbearable racket - Sophie was now totally panicked.

"What`s going on?" she yelled at the top of her voice; then almost as quickly as it started, everything dramatically stopped.

Sophie slowly released her grip on her ears and began to open her eyes; she was very aware that the intense noise could return any moment. As the ambient sounds and bright artificial light started to flood back into her perception, she quickly realised that her immediate surroundings had altered back to the studios.

"Have I been day-dreaming?" she asked herself. Sophie was still seated, but instead of the rickety table of hut 104, her legs were crossed under the reception counter-top, the desk in its usual shambolic state, stretched out before her. Pens and bits of paper lay strewn across the entire surface; a newspaper lay open just within Sophie's reach. She looked down at herself; her RAF uniform had been replaced by modern mufti and the strained noises of bands practising wafted up the corridor. Mr. Johnson was walking through reception carrying a large cardboard box and from what Sophie could make out, it was full of vinyl `LP` records. As she began to re-adjust to this alternative environment, Johnson spoke continuing on from the conversation he started in 1944.

"Bloody diversions! How much longer will they be?" he said, reiterating his annoyance. "Three weeks now I've had to lug my stuff all the way from Canal Street."

With this one sentence Sophie was totally thrown off her guard; she slowly assessed the facts and questions started to form in her mind.

"How did he know what we were talking about in the POW camp? Was I ever in a POW camp? Maybe I'm not actually in hospital, comatose?" The realisation of this possibility suddenly hit her.

"Bloody Hell! I'm just sitting at work, bored stupid making up all these fantasies just to kill time." The logic was sound; Johnson must have been talking to her while she was daydreaming - his voice leaching into her sub-consciousness and forming part of the banter. Sophie practically ran the studio, but she was so efficient that the day to day processes only took an hour or so, which left plenty of time to drift off to wherever her imagination wanted to go. Now, resigned to the fact that she was essentially at work and not off on a historical jaunt, Sophie finally acknowledged Johnson's presence.

"Hi, Mr. J. Sorry I was miles away."

"Just like bloody Canal Street!" Clearly he was frustrated and was struggling with the hefty box of records. As he staggered towards Sophie she could see what was going to happen and just managed to whip her newspaper away from underneath the incoming box.

"Terrific!" thought Sophie, "of all the realities I could be in, I've landed in the one with a grumpy customer and bleeding awkward boss."

As if waiting in the wings for his cue, the door swung open and Bob walked through, in an abnormally buoyant mood.

"Morning Soph." he said, almost with a smile which for Bob was positively radiant. It didn't last long, he looked at Johnson and his almost-smile melted away. "Morning." he mumbled, just about managing to string the two syllables together. Whilst avoiding eye contact with Johnson, Bob noticed the unwieldy box on the counter.

"What have you got there?"

"My album collection." Johnson replied with an element of pride. "I was clearing out the loft and found this lot; forgot I had them." He looked in Sophie's direction and continued. "Thought this youngster might want to hear what proper music sounds like." He threw a wink at Sophie.

"Cheeky git!" she said with a wry smile across her face; despite Johnson being cranky moments earlier, she understood he was only joking. Sophie enjoyed these little connections with her tutor, however the moment was soon lost when Bob addressed them both.

"Talking of proper music, I'm on the scrounge for a set of bagpipes."

"Why?" Sophie asked the question, but really didn't care, she picked up the newspaper and began to casually scan the pages for something interesting to read. Bob started to sort through the collection of rubbish on the desk; he replied without looking up.

"I'm being forced to observe another twelve months have passed since I last managed, not to forget our wedding anniversary." Throughout all the years Sophie knew them both, Bob rarely had a positive word to say about his wife; instinctively she would take his rants with a bucket of salt and side with Mrs. Marsh - knowing all too well how difficult living with Bob could be. However, Sophie was curious and thought she should show some vague interest in this proclamation; if nothing else she might influence Bob`s plans to ensure Mrs. Marsh had a relatively enjoyable evening, despite the inclusion of bagpipes.

"When is it?" she enquired. Bob appeared to go a bit misty eyed.

"Next week. I want to give her an evening to remember." Sophie was thrown slightly, he genuinely sounded like he was really trying to pull out all the stops; however given his past history she was a little unsure. Against her better judgement, the benefit of doubt was applied - she thought carefully, trying to compose her most compassionate sentence before delivering it with as much empathy as she could muster.

"That's nice." she eventually said. There was a pause while her brain put in for over-time, working out how to enhance what she thought was a solid start; finally she continued. "Nothing says; `Happy Anniversary` better than a soppy song played on the bagpipes." She was content this had fleshed out the sentiment enough and left the door open for Bob to respond along the same lines; possibly even reveal his true feelings. He stopped shuffling papers and looked up.

"Well quite. She makes me feel all rheumatic." Johnson, who was stood by the counter flicking through his records piped up.

"Don't you mean romantic?"

"I know *exactly* what I mean." muttered Bob through clenched teeth and with an element of disdain. As Bob was standing, facing away from the front desk, Johnson didn't properly hear him, but Sophie did. She now realised the leopard not only hadn't changed its spots, the claws were being sharpened in readiness to inflict an evening of misery, disappointment and bagpipes. Bob turned towards Johnson and continued.

"I`m also thinking of booking a trip for her."

"That sounds like a nice idea; anywhere good?" Johnson responded innocently - Sophie knew what was coming.

"Yes - did you see that news feature about the mission to colonise Mars?" Mr. J looked confused as Bob`s true colours were at last back on display. Sophie felt the need to interject.

"Seriously, you have to mark the occasion somehow. Where are you taking her?" she asked for clarification. Momentarily, Bob considered the advantages of a single, one way ticket to another planet, but like everything else it boiled down to cash-flow. He resigned himself to the fact that the budget wouldn't stretch that far and instead became engrossed by Johnson's record collection; picking up a handful of LP`s he started to read the sleeve notes. Sophie spoke again.

"Come on, where are you going?"

"Muplins holiday camp." Bob replied without looking up.

"In Clacton? Isn't that a converted POW camp?" Bob nodded, at which point a light went on in Sophie`s head.

"Hang on, I think there was an offer in the paper for Muplins." Sophie skimmed back a few pages in the local rag glancing over the print to recall where she had seen the ad.

"Here it is." Helpfully, she angled the paper slightly so Bob could read the small advert that nestled among the editorials. He barely glanced up from the very small print on the reverse of a Tom Jones album.

"Where?" he vaguely enquired.

"Here..!" Sophie tapped the page with vigour, annoyed that he was so disinterested. "...in between an article about a missing cat, and a message from the Sexual Health Advisory Group." She could tell he was only going through the motions of the conversation - his lips moved in time with his brain as he concentrated on the information about who made the tea for Mr. Jones. Finally, he decided to throw her an ounce of attention.

"What does it say?"

Sophie thought she would test Bob to see if he was actually paying attention.

"The `S-H-A-G` are holding a free consultation morning on..." Bob suddenly became attuned to Sophie`s words and hurriedly interrupted.

"No, I meant the money off deal." Sophie herself, had now become distracted by an adjacent article and unintentionally gave Bob a taste of his own medicine - she only just managed to respond.

"Twenty percent off, when you book online." Her voice tailed off as she quickly returned to the write up, her eyes travelling across and down the column absorbing the details as they unfolded. She finished and looked up.

"That's terrible." she said out loud, but Bob was still one conversation behind.

"Sounds a good deal to me." he said from within a pile of records. He hadn't realised the topic of conversation had moved on and his lack of comprehension deeply frustrated Sophie - she began to feel tense and slightly fuzzy in the head.

"Why does he have to be so bleeding obtuse?" she thought, as the mist continued to descend across her mind. Standing up and pushing her chair back, she chastised him for being inadvertently insensitive.

"Not the ad! The missing cat!" she snapped. Momentarily Bob felt hurt - this unjustifiable outburst had arrived from nowhere and he tried to work out where he had gone wrong. To reinforce her point, Sophie re-read the passage out loud.

"It says here; ex-serviceman, Jimmy Radmore; ninety seven, was shot down and captured on three different occasions, but each time escaped by tunnelling out of the camp." She paused to check that Bob was paying attention, then carried on. "He was seeing out his retirement with his only companion - Tom, his black and white cat. But, three weeks ago the veteran's pet went AWOL leaving Jimmy all alone." Sophie looked at Bob. "That's so sad."

"Maybe it tunnelled out?" suggested Bob, who seemed impervious to emotions of a sensitive nature. "If I were him, I would check the litter tray - probably got a false bottom." Sophie ignored his misplaced humour and carried on translating the text for the benefit of anyone who was actually listening.

"Looks like the paper is launching an appeal..."

As she carried on reading, once again her head became fuzzy and the print of the newspaper started to blur – suddenly without warning the words began to dance around on the page. She stopped - blinked a few times, the typeset quickly re-arranged itself back into the correct order and her address continued.

"...help us, help this war hero, and find Tom..."

The words suddenly took off across the page and disappeared. Sophie looked up from the now, blank page to find the room spinning around - she was perfectly still - everything else was a blur. The whirlwind intensified – outwardly Sophie remained calm as if this was a perfectly natural occurrence, but internally her mind churned round and round like a concrete mixer, blending thoughts embedded in reality with ideas conceived from fiction - trying to make sense of the chaos that surrounded her.

"Maybe, I'm not just bored at work…" As she considered this further, the spinning objects around her reached terminal velocity and began to distort from their recognisable forms – colours and shapes blurred until they became one big liquefied gloop, then like water running out a bath - the whole schmear was sucked into a vortex that originated from an epicentre, over by where a filing cabinet once stood. Only one object survived this bizarre storm – Sophie's chair remained fixed to the spot just behind her. Dazed and confused she quickly sat down - as the weight of her body made contact, in an instant the maelstrom abated and Sophie's vision came back into focus.

She was back in hut 104, seated at the rickety table.

* * *

Sophie took a moment - adjusting to her change of surroundings. The hut was as exactly as before; the cold night air floated up through the floor boards which made her thankful that the RAF-issue overcoat and thick socks had also returned. Bob had disappeared and the playing cards dealt by Johnson lay face down ready to be picked up - he sat across the table and had just finished sorting his hand, tutting at every revealed card.

"What a bally awful hand. Hope yours is better, WingCo?"

Sophie collected her allocated cards and thought hard about what to say next.

"How are those tunnels coming along?" seemed an appropriate question - after all she had placed herself in charge of the great escape. Suddenly the door of the hut flew open - a rather troubled and wheezing Knobby thundered in bringing more of the evening's icy atmosphere with him. Dressed in a rather dishevelled Flight Lieutenant`s uniform, he fought to get his words out between attempts to catch his breath.

"Sir! They've found Tom."

"What, the missing cat?" Sophie`s mind hadn`t quite lined up properly with the change in environment.

"No Sir. The Goons have found `Tom`."

She swiftly found Knobby`s wavelength and replied with in a confident voice.

"Got it - the tunnels. As in 'Tom', 'Dick' and 'Harry'."

It was a total guess, but Knobby`s reaction confirmed she was spot on.

"When did this happen?" she demanded – re-asserting her authority.

"Not sure, Sir." Knobby removed his hat and began to pass it nervously between his fingers.

"I thought all the tunnels were safe." Sophie ramped up the interrogation. "What the hell were the lookouts doing?" She was now totally absorbed in her role causing the hat-spinning to become faster.

"Don't know, Sir." Knobby's shoulders dropped and the grilling intensified.

"What about 'Harry' and 'Dick' - are they still under wraps?"

"Err, I'm not really in the loop on that one." he mumbled, knowing he was in all sorts of trouble. "Sorry Sir."

Sophie threw her cards across the table.

"For an `intelligence` officer, you really don't know a bleedin` lot."

Knobby couldn't really argue with this sentiment, but tried anyway.

"I did manage discover there is a new moon next week, Sir. Vital information I think you would agree."

"Hardly cutting edge - a cave dweller from Neolithic times could have told me about lunar phases. Honestly, between you and Bob 'the Scrounger' Marsh, it's a wonder we're getting anywhere. Talking of which, have you seen that walking liability recently?"

Sophie knew there was one character missing from this charade and assumed he would turn up at some point.

"I saw him earlier, by the mess hall." Knobby piped up, grateful the heat was on someone else. "He seemed excited about something - said he was off to see his contact."

"I hope it was to do with finding more civilian clothing."

"Oh yes - I was going to ask about that..." Knobby relaxed a little more. "...The costumes for the concert party are looking a bit thin on the ground."

"There not for your bloody pantomime!" For some reason, Knobby was really annoying Sophie - normally they were amicable, but currently he was really going against the grain. She got up and paced around the confined area - then stopped, spun round to face him.

"I'm planning to put fifty men the other side of that fence..." she said, vaguely pointing to outside. "...they need to blend in with their surroundings – be invisible. So far I've been presented with three bear costumes and a Widow Twanky outfit."

"Bob's trying his best." Knobby clearly felt the need to defend his fellow, lower ranked officer - but really should have known better.

"I'm prepared to be proved wrong." Sophie went on. "But personally I think the Gestapo are going to notice Robin Hood and his merry men attempting to board the midnight train to Frankfurt."

The tension was broken by a knocking on the wooden door – not a straight forward knock - it was long and convoluted - full of awkward gaps. All three looked at each other quizzically; there was a longer pause then the tapping started again from the beginning. Sophie couldn't allow the incessant drumming to continue.

"Can somebody get that, please?" she asked with an air of expectant dread. Knobby was nearest - he un-latched the hook and opened the door. Sophie wasn't overly surprised to see 'the scrounger' stroll in -dressed in a lowly Flying Officer's uniform - true to form - Bob held the junior rank.

"Hello Sir." he said cheerfully. "Sorry I can't salute." Sophie could see why - Bob had a set of bagpipes under one arm, while the other was tangled up in the ribbon holding the drones together.

"What the hell was all that banging?" she asked.

"The secret knock, Sir." Bob announced smugly, which did nothing to endear him to Sophie. She was now starting to get cross.

"We've never had a secret knock!"

"Is that so?" Bob replied. "I thought we did…" his voice tailed off.

Sophie could tell the forthcoming conversation was not going to go well – however, she persevered with low expectations.

"Tell me you have good news on the clothing front."

"I have good news and some, not so good news."

"Go on." Sophie mentally set the bar a notch lower.

"Ok, so my contact said some overcoats will be available by tomorrow, but the problem is she only has them in sizes ten and twelve."

"What colour?' Sophie instinctively enquired.

"Well - they are from last season's collection, so mainly grey and pink."

"Sounds good to me." she said excitedly - momentarily, Sophie had overlooked her setting. A sharp blast of cold air from under the hut, shot through the warped floorboards and quickly brought her current reality back into focus. She paused to take stock of the situation - the entire scenario was bordering on the bizarre - however there was an obvious and extraneous matter that needed to be given priority.

"Bob. Why do you have a set of bagpipes?" Instead of answering directly, as usual he waffled, imparting only circumstantial information.

"I scrounged them from a guard in the front gate house."

"Herr Wilhelm MacDougal?" Johnson immediately perked up and joined the conversation. "I know him - swiped his ID papers to copy."

The escape committee had recently appointed Johnson as the official forger, not for any ability to replicate material - more because he looked a bit like Donald Pleasance. Sophie rolled her eyes upwards and turned her attention towards Johnson.

"I've been meaning to talk to you about that."

"No need to offer praise sir - just doing my job." Johnson had totally missed the darker tone in her voice. "I thought they looked tip-top." he boasted.

"There's nothing wrong with their appearance; no-one could tell they are fake - unless of course they were in the same room." she said, raising the sarcasm level. "My problem is; you went to a lot of trouble to copy the official stamps etc. but the names you came up with could have been more in-keeping with the whole - trying to be German -thing."

Johnson gave a bemused shrug as Sophie slid open a drawer from under the table, reached to the back and pulled out the offending papers. Studying them, she continued.

"I think we might struggle to get to Switzerland pretending to be Herbert Joseph McBurnside, or Horst Gunter Von Inverurie."

Bob interrupted.

"Actually I thought these would make excellent bellows." He said, holding up the bagpipes. "...to pump fresh air down the tunnels to the lads." Finally - he had answered Sophie's initial question, it had taken him all this time to formulate a reason. The Wing Commander, having given it some thought, returned her attention back to him.

"Blimey, that's not such a bad idea."

Praise wasn't something Bob was used to in life and didn't really know how to react; he began to enjoy the acclaim but it was short lived...

"Sorry to barge in, Sir." Johnson interrupted - he didn't want Bob to have the spotlight for too long. "What are we going to do about Tom?" Sophie refocused.

"Ah yes, the tunnel. Who was digging at the time?" Johnson knew the answer wasn't going to be well received. He took a gulp.

"I'm afraid it was Stiltz, Sir." Sophie glanced despondently at the floor.

"Stiltz? The Cooler King?" He was brilliant at tunnelling and a great leader of men; Sophie knew that without him the operation would be set back. "What happened?" she enquired.

"Apparently he lost his bearings." Johnson continued. "Started digging up instead of along – ended up in the Camp Commandant's vegetable patch. Bad show, what?"

"Tad unfortunate." Sophie agreed.

"The C.O. happened to be digging for potatoes at the time; bent down to pick up a handful of King Edwards and found Stiltz looking up at him." Sophie winced. "He did his best to look like just another potato, but German brass are trained to spot these things."

Sophie barely heard him, she was thinking of how this would play out and, more importantly, how it would affect her own chances of escaping the incarceration of her hospital bed. She had already decided the time was right to return to normal life, where she could go to work, have a row with Bob, go to gigs and laugh with the others; but most of all, go home and give her mum a hug whenever she wanted. Emotions were bubbling under the surface but she had to fight them to remain calm and in control. Her own destiny was at stake.

"Where have they taken Stiltz?" she asked, her voice quivering slightly.

"To the cooler, Sir."

Sophie expected this and had already started to move towards the window; she swept the drab, makeshift curtain to one side and peered out. Sure enough, Stiltz was making his way towards the isolation hut, flanked by four guards. Despite facing a few days in the slammer and still smothered head to toe in earth, he walked with an arrogant swagger, down the well-trodden path to the cooler, nonchalantly pitching his trademark baseball into a worn leather glove with every step.

A few POW's had come out to give Stiltz a good send-off, and he acknowledged them with a smile. As he passed Taffy Ingram, the Welshman broke ranks and met the party outside the perimeter gate while the lead guard removed the padlock and chain. Taffy whistled -they all spun round and the Cooler King caught his eye; ignoring the sentries his fellow prisoner took a step forward and passed Stiltz his trombone, they nodded with mutual respect and the party carried on through the gate.

* * *

Sophie replaced the curtain, returned to the table and sat down – she knew Stiltz would be OK – he had his music to keep himself sane during the lonely days of solitary confinement, but it didn't help her cause. As she considered all options the sound of a mournful, blues trombone solo drifted over the distant night air.

"Damn!" She thumped the table dramatically. "He was one of our finest men." Johnson and Bob nodded in agreement.

"So, Sir, what do you suggest we do?" asked Knobby.

"Right! There is only one course of action." snapped Sophie – remembering she was in charge and moreover, she was British! "Let's have a cup of tea - stick the kettle on, there's a good chap."

Knobby shifted nervously, he didn't want to be the one pointing out the obvious, but clearly the boss had forgotten a vital piece of information. Sophie stared, waiting for a response.

"Can't do that Sir." Eventually, he spoke. "That stove is a dummy - it hides the entrance to `Cynthia`, Sir." Sophie slapped her forehead.

"Cynthia! I completely forgot about her - one of our earlier digging efforts. Remind me, how far down did the old girl get?" Knobby shuffled like a kid handing in overdue homework knowing his five hundred word essay was four hundred and ninety three words light.

"Well, at the last survey we'd cleared about four inches, Sir."

Sophie contemplated this fact.

"How thick are the floorboards in this hut?"

Knobby realised teacher was about to read a seven worded title then turn over to find a blank page.

"Around six inches, Sir."

"So, not really a tunnel - more a dent in the floor." The Wing Co.'s reaction could have gone in many directions; she chose the sarcastic route.

* * *

Sophie sensed that she was losing grip of this particular reality so she shook her head to clear the mist and stood up forcing her chair back, scraping it`s legs along the wooden floor. She was about to speak when she noticed a modern looking turntable had somehow appeared on the table in front of her; Johnson - who was minding his own business, flicked through a large box of records totally disregarding her. This strange turn of events neither phased nor worried Sophie, she simply accepted her reality was about to change again.

"I need to think; put a record on, old boy, it helps me concentrate."

Johnson obliged by selecting a random vinyl disc from the pile; pulling it out he inspected the front cover.

"Ah yes, here's one I think you will like."

He placed the needle in the first groove and flicked the switch, moments later the unmistakable sound of a seventies style funky guitar riff filled hut 104. As the bass and drums joined in, the toes and heads of the three men started to tap and nod respectively - unconsciously at first - but when eye contact was made it became a communal act - almost tribal as the funky rhythms awoke their dormant primal instincts.

All were moved by the music, except Sophie; unusually she wasn't really listening - her mind was elsewhere; the newspaper she read earlier had now re-appeared next to the record player - she drew her chair back into position and sat down. Turning over a fresh page, an article about a local charity trying to raise money for a donkey sanctuary caught her eye.

Johnson strutted across the hut towards the table and shouted at Sophie, trying to make himself heard above the record.

"Great groove eh?"

But Sophie wasn't in the mood, she closed her eyes and ears to shut out the sights and noises that affronted her senses - hesitated for a moment, then opened them again.

* * *

Chapter 5

Sophie continued to look down at the table - the newspaper lay open and the turntable in front of her continued to spin the same tune that played in the hut; as she started to take note of her environment, reality dawned - she was back in the reception area of the studios once more, and all present were dressed in civvies. Bob, Johnson and Knobby were occupied, sifting through and playing records on decks the latter had brought with him.

Sophie wondered how long she had actually been daydreaming; the pile of records they had already listened to had built up, so she reckoned her mind had been elsewhere for a while. She readjusted the chair, but kept a low profile hoping that no one noticed her lack of attention.

* * *

The newspaper was full of the usual haphazard stories and editorials; the theft of a ladder, gig listings for the local music scene, an eclectic job section filled with employers seeking apprentices for weird commercial ventures.

While Sophie scanned down the print the others continued to get excited about music from another lifetime; with every album that Bob flicked through, he passed comment - reminiscing about its first airing, or that he saw the band once at some grotty, long closed down venue. Occasionally he would break off from his nostalgia rush to suggest Sophie listen to an obscure track to get fresh ideas for her band. His words simply blended in with the non-descript choice of music.

"I would rather listen to paint dry." Sophie retorted - she was currently in a very grumpy mood, but Bob was too distracted to notice; emotions were being stirred as he recalled earlier parts of his life from which these tunes formed the soundtrack.

"Yup, had this one; bought it from Woolworths with my first wage packet." His eyes lit up as each vinyl nugget was revealed.

"Oh wow - amazing! One of my all-time favourites. Ella Fitzgerald!" Again he felt the need to share his discovery with Sophie. "Hey, look at this."

"Mmmm ...what?" she mumbled without looking up - her acknowledgement was brief and indifferent.

"Ella Fitzgerald!" repeated Bob.

"Does she; lucky Gerald." replied Sophie, swiftly returning to the paper - however her concentration was soon to be shattered. Bob casually passed by a few more albums; suddenly, he froze.

The covers had started to blend in with one another and his brain was becoming overloaded with memorabilia, however one very specific, colourful piece of artwork passed within his view and he instantly recognised it as a record by his all-time favourite artiste. Bob become very animated.

"Bloody Hell!" he exploded. Sophie jumped, as did the needle on the record player as he planted both hands firmly on the desk. To confirm his initial thoughts, slowly he pulled out from within the stack a disc that resonated with him more than any other. He handled it with the same reverence and awe as an archaeologist would treat an exceptional artefact.

"Where did you get this?" he asked. "I've been trying to find a copy for years." Knobby and Johnson were a little taken aback by Bob's over-reaction, but he did appear truly overwhelmed to be holding a pristine copy of an album from his youth.

"Which one is it?" asked Mr. J, who was round the other side of the counter. Rather than give a straight answer, Bob continued reflecting on its provenance in his gushing, enthusiastic manner.

"Only the greatest album from the nineteen-seventies..."

Sophie considered this to be a major claim, she knew of several classic recordings making their debut in that decade and couldn't understand why Bob had singled out this particular one. Still feeling a little cranky she wanted to burst Bob's bubble.

"Is it Art Garfunkel's greatest hits?" was her flippant response.

"No! But thank you for finally taking an interest." replied Bob.

"What have you found?" repeated Johnson.

Bob wasn't avoiding the question on purpose, he just wanted the small gathering of music lovers to understand the enormity of this find; the fact that Johnson had already found the record ages ago, appeared to have passed him by. He went on imparting his limitless knowledge.

"Many of your, so called modern musicians' say this guy was their biggest influence..." Bob drivelled on like a highly emotional train spotter. "...without this gift to the world of music, current performers wouldn't be anything."

"Is it Perry Como?" Sophie asked in a facetious tone.

Bob was getting frustrated – this album meant a lot to him and Sophie obviously wasn't taking it seriously. Going slightly red in the face he finally put the record straight.

"I'm talking about the legend that is Curtis Muff."

Sophie blinked.

"Curtis what?"

"Muff." repeated Bob. "His first album, 'Sidewalk Spit' took the industry by storm; recorded during the summer of '76." Bob went a little misty eyed.

Sophie wet the tip of her finger and nonchalantly used it to turn the next page of the paper.

"Never heard of him." she said.

"Call yourself a musician!" Bob was indignant at Sophie's dismissive attitude. "Muff paved the way for all the rap, hip- hop and acid jazz stars that are around today." With this outburst he became even more animated - Sophie couldn't have looked more disinterested, but the lecture continued.

"He started out playing sessions for soul legends like, Otis Slough..."

"Who?" Sophie interrupted him.

"Come on, Soph! You must have heard of him." She had, but simply shrugged her shoulders innocently just to be irritating. Bob blundered on.

"He had that famous hit - Sitting on the side of the dock."

Sophie continued to play dumb to annoy Bob further, but he was so wrapped up in trying to get his message across, he failed to pick up on her endeavours.

"Maybe you will be aware of his contemporaries." he ventured, trying to expand the context. "Wilson Pocket? Little Stevie Ponder? Marvin Straight?"

"Marvin Straight?" Sophie frowned.

"You know, they used his most famous tune on that advert"

"Which one?"

"Cat food, I think..."

Sophie had succeeded in tying Bob`s mind in knots. Now, well and truly side tracked he cleared his throat and resumed the position of lecturer.

"Anyway - Curtis Muff played with all these guys, cutting his teeth, learning the trade - grafting to hone his skills." Bob adopted a more dramatic tone. "Then, suddenly he disappeared! Six months went by with no-one knowing where he was..."

Sophie turned another page of the paper and sighed.

"But, when he came back from oblivion, he had produced a phenomenal solo album which was this, definitive, mould-breaking master piece."

His voice reached a crescendo as he held up the immaculate copy of `Sidewalk Spit`, as if presenting the final and conclusive piece of evidence to a jury. His closing speech was passionate, endeavouring to prove, unequivocally that Muff was guilty of nothing more than simply being a genius.

"Hang on...Curtis Muff?" Sophie suddenly lifted her head up from the paper. "That name does ring a bell."

Bob was really pleased with himself - he had awoken some dormant piece of information in Sophie`s mind with his boundless enthusiasm.

"I knew you would have heard of him."

Sophie had a recollection, but not for the reasons Bob thought.

"Now I think about it, I recently took a booking for a jam session under that name." She swivelled her chair round to face the PC and nudged the mouse to wake it up. After a few clicks she was able to confirm her suspicions. "There you are - a booking for the eighteenth." She glanced up at the wall calendar. "That's next week."

Bob's pulse started to race, he could hardly believe what he was hearing - not only had a slice of his youth just been unearthed - his long-time hero was going to grace them with his presence.

"Muff is coming here? To my studios!"

It was Johnson who finally asked the question that was in the minds of everyone else in the room.

"Why?"

Sophie's brain raced back and forth, something else regarding this character was logged in there somewhere.

"Hang on a mo." She hurriedly grabbed the newspaper and scanned down, across and along the pages finally spotting, buried deep in the gig listings the details she was looking for.

"I thought so - the nineteenth - for one night only. 'The Tunneler's' pub is proud to present - Curtis Muff and his band."

Bob racked his brain to think of reasons to justify this revelation; then the penny dropped and he got very excited again.

"His people must have wanted a rehearsal place closest to the venue."

Knobby had been listening to the conversation but couldn't quite fit the pieces together; acting as the voice of reason he posed the obvious question that appeared to have eluded Bob.

"Why would an international recording star be gigging around here?"

It was a fair question and for a moment Bob's world imploded; he was so desperate for it to be true, but validation was required. A justifiable and lucid reason for this unusual event needed to be found.

"Maybe he is doing a few, low key warm up sessions before he hits the big venues?" It sounded like a reasonable argument but the blank look on his colleague's faces told him they weren't convinced – more was needed. "All musicians have to practice, that's why I'm in business; why not `Caramel Two` studios?"

He glanced at the others for approval, but the vacant looks continued. More propaganda was required, he reached out with both hands and clutched as many straws as possible.

"They all do it." he stuttered. "Madonna once played the 'Coach and Horses' in the high street." He delivered this with so much confidence he nearly convinced himself it was true. But not the others.

A stony silence filled the room.

Sophie contemplated her options; she could continue to goad Bob – which was fun... or prop up his argument with a supportive message. Being a dreamer herself she felt there was a sort of kinship between them, so decided to offer a sympathetic nod towards his esoteric ramblings.

"So, you boys off to see this Muff bloke then?"

Bob was relieved that someone had finally bought into his fantasy and happily continued.

"Try and stop me." he said cheerfully. In his haste, however he hadn't fully made the connection; Sophie had - and done the maths.

"I won't, but Mrs Marsh will - it's your anniversary on the nineteenth."

She may as well have told Bob that both his legs would have to come off; he had been riding high on adrenalin, thinking the moment was coming that he could see a legend in action, only to have it cruelly taken away by the prospect of having to take the wife out instead.

"Bugger - I forgot about that." He slumped down in the chair. "I can't miss this gig."

Johnson had been quiet for a while, but decided it was time to restore the status quo between Bob and himself. Although they had shared a little common ground over the LP's, he couldn't and shouldn't let this get in the way of their usual loathing for each other. The knife had already been innocently buried between his shoulder blades by Sophie; it was time to give it a twist.

"So, looks like you're going to miss the big gig; unless you have an escape plan? Any ideas?"

"I don't know; dig a tunnel, perhaps?" Bob sounded dejected and knew the options were scarce.

Sophie started to feel a little uneasy with the way the conversation was heading, she felt an empathy with Bob, and although they argued a lot seeing him be pounced upon and his dream shattered, was something that made her uncomfortable.

* * *

The temperature of the room had slowly been rising and Sophie`s head was feeling on the light side; fresh air was needed. She made her excuses and headed for the front door; nearing the main entrance she looked back to check Bob was ok. He had gone back to flicking through the records, but this time with not as much gusto or passion. Sophie was about to move on when Bob pulled out a vinyl disc from its sleeve and placed it on the deck; he looked at Sophie and smiled as the needle clicked into the groove and the warm sound of the pre-track hiss filled the speakers. She smiled back at him and turned to leave, feeling that at least he had recovered some happiness from another record. Her hand clasped the handle and pressing down she released the catch and opened the door.

As she did, two slightly strange things happened; first, her ears detected the sound of Bob`s record starting up from within the reception area. She knew his taste in music fairly well, but didn't expect to hear the faint strains of bagpipes in the background – a relatively odd choice she thought. The second, took Sophie more by surprise; as she stepped through the door, instead of finding herself in the street avoiding the road works, she now stood outside hut 104 staring out across an exercise yard and over to the small allotment where fellow POW`s were working the land.

She blinked a few times expecting the scene to disappear and be replaced by traffic cones, traffic wardens...maybe traffic? Nothing changed; once again she had involuntary donned an RAF uniform and her fellow prisoners were looking at her to lead them to freedom.

* * *

Chapter 6

Alone, Sophie wandered slowly across the yard pondering her destiny, thoughts passing through her mind at a rate that was difficult to process. In better times her mind was prolific, conjuring up philosophies often as a result of misinterpreting situations; this slight twisting of her immediate reality gave rise to fantastic concepts that were often oddly peculiar and other times peculiarly odd, but always very entertaining.

But now she wanted a clear understanding to why her musings had become increasingly surreal. The long walk across the compound gave her ample time to talk herself through the quandaries.

"Maybe I am simply sitting at work with too much coffee and time on my hands?" It took a few more paces to digest this notion, but she knew in her heart this wasn't right. "Can't be, my thoughts are too scrambled, even for me." Sophie glanced to her right and noticed an Alsatian lighting a cigarette as its handler took a pee up the side of a hut. She reached a conclusion.

"I'm definitely lying in a comatose state; my body is frozen in time, but my mind is free." Sophie was satisfied with this explanation; her intense imagination, unbound by any restrictions was a trade-off for being imprisoned in her own body.

* * *

The allotment was now only a few steps away; she had passed fellow airmen scattered randomly around the yard, some sitting crossed legged playing board games, others trying to find the energy to stretch muscles that had become weary through lack of use - much like her own. She stopped to take stock.

"I know these guys don't really exist, but in a funny sort of way, in my head, they do."

She looked around at her immediate companions - as she studied them closely the realisation dawned; all prisoners, large or small in stature, carrying an injury, or fighting fit; each and every one had an identical face: Hers!

Sophie's breath was taken away and she dropped to her knees - it was so strange seeing herself many times over and her brain strained to cope with this concept. After a moment of intense thinking, suddenly her mind found a clear and simple explanation – collectively the clones all represented her and by committing to help these imaginary prisoners, without realising they had given her the motivation to keep battling for survival.

She jumped to her feet – suddenly invigorated by this revelation.

"If I just sit around waiting for the war to finish – I'm never going to make it." She looked at her alter egos. "We've got to get out of here."

* * *

It was Flight Lieutenant Knobby who broke Sophie's concentration, shouting not to her, but at Bob as he passed the allotment.

"Finished that tunnel yet?" he said cheerily.

"Shhhh! Keep your voice down!" Bob reacted angrily to the intrusive question. Knobby could be a little naïve at times and shrunk into his shoulders, realising his mistake. Whispering, he tried to make amends.

"Sorry, the guards. I forgot."

"I'm more worried about the wife finding out." said Bob.

Overhearing this out-of-context comment made Sophie smile; she adopted her RAF style of delivery and addressed both men in hushed, but commanding tones.

"Right Chaps, debrief in two minutes. Don't be late." She turned to address Knobby. "Have you heard from the council about planning permission for the third tunnel?" His reaction spoke volumes as he remained clueless about most aspects of the escape.

"Err, I couldn`t get hold of building control, Sir." Sophie shot him a glance which made him re-think his answer. "I`ll try again."

Sophie had found her stride once more!

"You do that; can't afford any more problems. I've already had health and safety on my back this week - apparently we should all have hi-vis jackets on."

"Bleeding red-tape!" replied Knobby as he wondered off in the direction of the hut, leaving Sophie bemused to why she had abstractly made the POW camp subject to modern day building regs. Just then, an anxious looking Bob sidled up to her and spoke, his voice quivering slightly and charged with emotion.

"Sir, what are the chances of you making it?"

Normally Bob was a brash individual, but now displayed a trait that she hadn't associated with him before. Sophie, as a superior officer, felt a responsibility to allay his fears but also genuine compassion towards his timid demeanour.

"It`s going to happen; I`m getting out of here one way or another and I'm taking you lot with me." She gave a reassuring smile and concluded, "Everything *will* be ok." This coda was more to reinforce her own convictions, but it also helped Bob calm his nerves.

"Thank you, Sir" His deep concerns about Sophie`s escape had been lifted - heartened by her fighting spirit he wanted more details.

"So, how long before the big push?"

It was a fair question but Sophie realised there was still a long way to go; once again the tunnels become her focus.

"Not sure, Bob. It would help if we could get rid of the waste soil quicker...we need more volunteers for the old `earth down the trouser leg` and `stamp it in`, routine." Bob acknowledged this with a smile and nodded into the distance over Sophie`s shoulder.

"Looks like that guy over there is doing his bit."

Sophie spun around to see her physician, Doctor Strange, now adorning the uniform of an Air Marshal. He was pacing up and down the allotment while surreptitiously emptying great clods of earth from within his trouser legs. Fellow workers followed him, quickly raking over the ground to disguise the freshly excavated soil.

"There you go, even your top man is helping." said Bob.

Sophie paused. He was right, her doctor was clearly trying to help her escape from captivity, albeit not the physical confines of barbed wire and armed guards, but the esoteric entrapment of a coma. She felt positive about the situation, more than ever before, knowing that all around were fighting her corner every step of the way; even Bob. Maybe she had misjudged him? Feeling closer to him than she had ever felt, she wanted to know more about his background.

"What made you join the RAF, Bob?" He didn't have to think about this for long; his emotions bubbled to the surface again and he gazed into the distance.

"To travel; see the world, but I didn't think I would end up in this hell hole." His focus switched directly to Sophie. "If I wanted to be surrounded by barbed wire, sleep in rows of wooden huts and be forced to follow a strict regime, I would have booked a week at Muplins holiday camp." He winked. "Still it could be worse..."

"How?" Sophie responded.

"The wife could be here."

Things were slowly getting back to how they should be and Sophie took this as a positive sign that normality was being restored.

* * *

A solitary bell chimed in the far corner of the camp; all that heard it knew they only had minutes to return to the confines of their huts; lockdown was approaching. They walked at a pace to meet the deadline and entered the hut just as the last peal was dying away.

`104` had been designated HQ for the escape committee and as such only personnel involved were admitted. Knobby and Johnson were busy doing nothing as Sophie and Bob entered; she was now fired up and meant business.

"Right gents; the big push. Today is the 18th and our un-intelligence officer has calculated a new moon is due, so the ambient light will be minimal. The tunnel is now finished, so I think we should make a break for it tomorrow night."

"Which tunnel are we going to use Sir?" asked Johnson.

"Well, as you know the Goons found Tom; as far as Harry goes…" She hesitated, "…let's just say there were issues." Sophie really didn't want to go into details and was ready to move on, but Johnson had already shot a disdainful glance towards Bob, who now stared at his shoes knowing full well what was coming.

"The main issue being that Bob was in charge." sneered Johnson.

"I did my best, given the circumstances." Came the reply, delivered with little conviction.

"Circumstances which include, you being in charge." Mr. J always thought Bob was the weak link and had let the side down. Despite looking adversity square on, the feeble defence continued.

"I thought I had some innovative ideas…"

"You had some bloody awful ones too." Johnson snapped. "Watching you dig a hole with a toilet brush because you thought it wouldn't make much noise was a personal highlight."

"I was right; it was practically silent."

"Silent, but as effective as trying to dig a hole with a toilet brush." He couldn't think of an appropriate simile, so went with the obvious. Sophie tried to continue her big speech but Johnson was now in full flow.

"Why didn't you use more conventional equipment?"

"I tried using a pneumatic drill, but got complaints about the noise from the chaps in `diversion and subterfuge`." Johnson saw another chasm open up in Bob`s armour and felt obliged to exploit it.

"And, who was in charge of D `n S?' he asked, knowingly. Bob had nothing. Johnson intensified the interrogation. "They were supposed to be vaulting over a horse; performing other gymnastics… Providing a distraction."

"Yes, but…"

"So, why did you make them play dominoes?" queried Johnson. "The gentle clicking together of small bits of wood with dots on, was hardly going to drown out the incessant racket coming from your hut."

"A few of the lads had notes asking for them to be excused." Bob reluctantly divulged. "...and I wanted to make everyone feel inclusive, so I went for a non-contact sport."

This enraged Johnson, a trait Sophie had never seen in him before. Her concern was, he was going too far with this witch hunt. A highly frustrated Mr. J spoke again.

"The idea of a distraction unit is to disguise the industrious sounds of tunnel construction, not to provide an after school club for non-sporty types. I'm surprised the Germans didn't hear the drilling!"

"They did - luckily our regimental mascot is the woodpecker, so we just blamed the noise on that."

Bob was satisfied he had managed to knock back that particular line of enquiry, but his lopsided logic was straightened with a simple and reasonable question from Johnson.

"What's wrong with using trowels, spades, shovels...?"

Sophie had heard enough, she realised this was just a slanging match between two old adversaries and had to take control of the situation. She stood up abruptly in order to bring the attention on herself and banged the table with her fist.

"Gentlemen!" she roared. "This isn't getting us anywhere."

Sophie had barely begun her rallying speech before it was hijacked, and now she would have to work twice as hard to unify the divided team; the whole escape could be jeopardised - inspirational words were definitely required.

"When our backs are against the wall we have to be creative and use whatever we can get our hands on. Remember, with a right tool, any job can be done."

"We had a right tool - he was in charge." said Johnson.

Sophie just wanted to knock their heads together, she desperately wanted to return to a healthy, normal life and wasn't going to let a couple of bickering idiots get in the way.

"Ladies please! As I was saying, Tom is out of commission, and Harry is a non-starter - so that leaves Dick."

Knobby was pleased the heated exchange had stopped and the topic returned to the job in hand, but he was a little slow on the uptake.

"I thought Dick was full of the excavated earth from Tom?" Sophie closed her eyes, sensing her pending escape slipping away. She sighed before going over details the others surely should already know.

"Pay attention this time! We put the soil from Tom in Mildred, Harry's soil went into Simone and Dick's was cunningly tipped into the duck pond." Knobby looked slightly perplexed.

"I didn't know there was a duck pond."

"There isn't any more." Sophie spoke through gritted teeth. "It's full of soil - we told the Germans it silted up."

"So, Dick it is then?" concluded Knobby.

Sophie felt like she was wading through porridge.

"Look, if we don't get a move on, the war will be over."

Blank faces continued to gawked at her and she realised more explanation was required.

"Not Dick - no. That tunnel had its own set of problems." She leant in toward the group and lowered her voice. "Unbeknown to us, the Americans were working on their own project. Three more tunnels; `Groucho, Harpo and Chico`, running east to west across the compound." Johnson looked puzzled.

"So what's the issue?" Sophie moved in even closer to signify the information she was about to impart was top secret.

"Dick was running north to south. Last week Chico and Harpo ran into Dick. We only found out when our lads bumped into a couple of Yanks coming the other way."

"But Sir, what about Groucho?" Johnson enquired.

"That was going great guns. They threw their best moles at it and worked round the clock."

"So, we're using that one?" said Johnson optimistically. Sophie desperately wanted to say `yes`, but she knew the news was going to take a turn for the worst.

"Sadly, not." Johnson`s face dropped, but not as much as Sophie`s hopes. "No one actually told them when to stop digging. They went down fifteen feet, across the compound, through the woods and kept going."

"And?" said Johnson.

"When they finally surfaced they found themselves in the P-O-W camp down the road." Bob was panicked by this news, his stiff upper lip had loosened while the knot in his stomach, tightened. Sophie shared his fears, but had to remain cool headed.

"So with our tunnels out of action and the American trio SNAFU, how are you getting out of here?" Bob asked, anxiously. There was an eerie silence within the room as the three subordinates looked at their leader for a motivating update. Sophie, remembering her mum`s words, delved deep into the recesses of her imagination to find inspiration and a positive outcome. Finally she spoke.

"Thankfully the Polish contingent have been working on a couple of tunnels for some months now; they start from inside the shower block."

Knobby`s face suddenly lit up as a moment of recognition was reached.

"I had noticed them keep going in and out the washrooms; I just assumed they had OCD." The news was optimistic but Johnson still demanded clarification.

"So, which tunnel are we using?"

"Alan." Sophie replied, selecting the first name that sprang to mind.

"Alan?" quizzed Johnson.

"Yes! Alan." Sophie was irritated about being questioned on her choice of made up name and wanted to swiftly move on to important details. "So, tomorrow night we need to rendezvous...."

"That`s no good, I'm afraid..." Frustratingly, her speech had been interrupted yet again. "The gang show opens on Saturday and tomorrow is our last rehearsal." said Knobby sounding very blasé. This totally wrong-footed Sophie - how could he possibly be concerned over a double booking at a time like this?

Sophie stared in disbelief; here she was trying to pull off one of the most daring escapes of the war and her Intel officer was prioritising some mediocre, tawdry showbiz folly. It was about to get worse.

"Thinking about it, we have bridge club on Thursdays." informed Johnson.

She looked at him, then Knobby and finally Bob and awaited his barmy excuse. In a nervous, semi-stuttered sentence he drove home the last nail.

"It's my wedding anniversary tomorrow - I have to take the wife out."

Sophie was furious and couldn't comprehend what the clowns around her were playing at!

"Why are you all throwing trivial, inconsequential obstacles in the way? Don't you realise - I'm trapped. I've got to get out of here!"

* * *

There was an uneasy atmosphere in the hut as awkward glances were exchanged. Sophie realised she had let her emotions take over and this had resulted in division and uncertainty - the absolute opposite of what she wanted or needed.

The void this created in Sophie's mind gradually filled as her mum's mantra again re-played on a loop throughout her head. It started in a distant corner - down a few corridors maybe on a different floor, she couldn't tell, but spread very quickly, echoing around the stark walls of her mind.

"Always react to any circumstance with a positive and measured response." - from beyond the horizon of Sophie's dreamscape, the sage advice was again delivered. Just like any concerned parent, her mum repeated the guiding words in hope the impetuous youth would finally take note. It had the desired effect - Sophie felt suitably reprimanded by the invisible force. She gave herself a metaphorical slap round the cheek and, wanting to make her mum proud, cleared her head so supressed positive thoughts could have unimpeded passage to the surface.

Slowly a way forward presented itself - an ambitious idea entered her mind; if she could change the context of her surroundings, it could force the outcome she wanted; after all it was how this adventure started in the first place.

"If it worked getting into this hell-hole, it may work in reverse?" she muttered to herself. All she had to do was think of a concept associated with a completely different scenario. Considering the options for a moment, Sophie smiled as a notion entered her head; she knew exactly what to say.

"Sorry Chaps, we can't discuss this any further; there isn't enough time." In an over-exaggerated manor, she pulled back her sleeve to glance at a wrist watch. "Curtis Muff is due in about ten minutes."

Bob immediately rose up, clattered into the table sending his chair flying; clearly he was agitated.

"Ten minutes! I'd totally forgotten about Muff; I'm not ready..." He began to blindly charge around the hut, arms flailing around like a conductor bringing Beethoven's Ninth to a conclusion while fighting a disgruntled wasp. Sophie hoped for a reaction, but didn't expect it to be quite so dynamic. Bob's behaviour started to become more eccentric than normal and all Sophie could do was try to keep out the way and observe.

It was when he started moving backwards with a degree of ferocity and with no regard for who or what was in his path that she became concerned.

"Calm down!" she yelled, but to no effect, Bob was far too busy rotating like a demented washing machine.

Then it happened.

Bob's manoeuvres were random in sequence and therefore difficult to predict; Sophie dodged to the right thinking this would avoid a collision, but midway through his trajectory he altered direction and velocity. The pair connected in an ungainly manner causing Sophie to reel back in shock, her eyes shut tight to block out the impending pain. It never came, Sophie opened her eyes and shouted once more.

"Will you cool it?" Even as the last word was still being formed in her mouth, she realised something had drastically changed.

"He's due in ten minutes, and I haven't got ready." Bob's words brought her mind into focus of where and when she now was. The group had returned to the reception area of the studio, Bob was still flapping around, not as vivaciously as before but still with an element of urgency. Sophie looked at him, them at the other two, finally down at herself.

* * *

The plan worked, she had forced her mind back to the reality of the present day and all its associated trappings. She had no pain where Bob made contact, just a slight headache which seemed to be with her most of the time anyway.

"Ready? How do you mean?" she asked.

"I haven't found a pen that works." said Bob as if it were an obvious problem. He feverishly grabbed at all available ball-points and scribbled in vein on anything he could find.

"Why do you need a pen?' asked a confused Sophie.

"I'm going to ask him to sign my album." Bob`s seemingly illogical actions now made sense, however a tetchy Mr. J now joined the conversation.

"He won't do that!"

"I'm sure he's an easy going chap." said Bob defensively, determined that nothing was going to spoil the moment he finally welcomes his hero to the studios.

"He won't sign *your* album, cos it *my* album."

Bob immediately saw the gravity of the situation. His arch rival was holding all the cards, but he simply had to have that record. To own a personalised autograph from this legend would be a high point of his life – not that there were many to compete with. Bob reined in his enthusiasm in order not to show off his true ambitions.

"Sorry I got carried away. I don't suppose you could let me have the LP? It would mean so much." Johnson paused - he was calculating something in his head which was obvious to Sophie; Bob on the other hand was too wrapped up in the fantasy of meeting his idol.

"I suppose I could let you have it for..." Johnson`s reply was interrupted.

"...Old time's sake? Thanks, mate." Bob`s pre-emptive wish sounded great in his head, but not so in Johnson`s. Assuming the deal could be sealed with a small sweetener, he concluded. "There's a drink in it for you."

"I was going to say, for two hundred." Johnson brought Bob crashing back to reality.

"Two hundred quid! That's a flipping big drink." Bob retorted as his heckles started to rise. Mr. J knew the strength of his bargaining position and continued to justify his reasoning.

"By your own admission, this was a very influential album. I think it's worth it."

"Still, that's a lot of money." Bob glanced at the clock on the wall and his pulse started to race. "Come on, he is due in nine minutes."

As soon as he announced this Johnson smirked and came straight back with another proposal.

"Nine minutes? Let's call it two-fifty then." Bob was now fairly red in the face; he could see the opportunity if a lifetime slipping away.

"That's outrageous!" he protested.

"Well, it's one of my favourite albums; I play it all the time."

The screws were turning.

"Played it all the time!" Bob was vexed. "Twenty four hours ago it was gathering dust in your attic, along with the Christmas decorations and your morals."

Just then the sound that Bob was dreading cut through the air like a fart at a funeral. The main door buzzer sounded. This could only mean one thing and Johnson felt duty bound to point it out.

"Sounds like the Muff-meister is a bit early."

The deal had yet to be done and Bob was seconds away from having nothing significant for the star to sign. He stood, frozen to the spot, gazing at the inner reception door waiting for his destiny to arrive. Johnson took this opportunity to introduce a new proposition; it wasn't really about the money it was more about watching Bob squirm.

"OK. Three hundred pounds for this famous and dare I mention, rare copy of `Sidewalk Spit`." He quickly fired this at Bob and concluded with a phrase which created a definitive, verbal full stop. "Final offer!"

Bob knew he was beaten but it didn't matter to him at this juncture, the record had to be his. He hurried over to the till, hit the button, and the tray sprung open to reveal its contents. Without any thought whatsoever, Bob grabbed a handful of notes that looked the right colour and thrust them into Johnson's hand, at the same time snatching the record from his grasp. The transaction was complete and not a moment too soon, the handle of the reception door dropped and all eyes fell on the entrance as they awaited the arrival of the celebrity.

* * *

Bob stared at the character that had just revealed himself; obviously he had an image in his head of how the legend would look after being out of the public eye for a few years and had prepared himself to meet an older version. However, the character that now stood before him certainly didn't look older. In fact, he appeared considerably younger than the photo of him on the album sleeve from the seventies. And then he spoke.

"Alright Homies? Me and m` crew have a room booked in this 'ere establishment for tonight, coz we is hitting the Tunneler's pub tomorrow wiv our sounds, innit."

Bob blinked, and looked down at the very expensive album cover then back up at the teenage pretender.

"Who the bloody hell are you?" He enquired. Curtis looked over the top of his shades and answered the question with another question.

"Are you disrespectin` me, Bruv?" Instantly the attitude was cranked up, while his already saggy trousers, drooped. "I'm Curtis Muff."

"No you're not!"

"Do you want to see m` driving license and `ting?"

84

"You're old enough to drive!?" Bob contested. "Sorry, I was expecting a nineteen-seventies singing legend - instead I get a reject from an early round of the `X` factor."

"`ang on, you're talking abou` the late, great Curtis Muff; my rents were big fans, that's why they named me after him."

Bob was stunned, not only had the delinquent heard of his hero the adolescent wannabee rapper, just imparted the news that said idol was in fact - deceased. And he had paid out three hundred pounds on an album that would remain bereft of an autograph. It took a moment to digest this information.

"Did you say late ....?" Bob whimpered.

* * *

Sophie watched this debacle unfold while tracking back through her memory banks to recall how this confusion could have begun; then recognition emerged from the haze that she had caused Bob`s all-consuming hysteria that ultimately cost him money. An exit strategy was required. Looking around, to her immediate left was a small box from which three wires protruded; she hadn't noticed it earlier. There was an obvious on-off switch at the front which Sophie felt compelled to flick down - as she did the gizmo sprung to life and began emitting a regular, annoying beep. Glaring at the machine the realisation slowly hit as to what it was - and the implications of it being present.

* * *

The heated debate about the dead singer continued in the foreground while a constant, undulating hum of bands rehearsing behind closed doors supplied the accompaniment. Sophie began to feel disengaged from this reality. Amidst this frenetic setting she could see lips moving and people loitering, yet while the mayhem developed around her, she just sat unable to interact and shrouded in isolation - just like a home economics teacher at parent`s evening. Incoherent sounds simply floated around before passing her by, slowly fading into an obscure distance.

The young pretender continued to speak; although Sophie still had him in plain sight he sounded as if he was in another room, wearing a balaclava. Bob too.

"Three hundred quid! Talking of death, Sophie! I want a word with you." He was only an arm's length away but his tones were almost imperceptible.

There was now only one sound Sophie was aware of; the machine at her side continued its monotonous, repetitive beep. She closed her eyes and everything faded away.

* * *

Chapter 7

Sophie lay on the bed, still conscious of the beeping monitor. Muff, Bob and the others were not on her horizon, but she was aware of another presence in the room. A voice spoke. Through a haze of memories she desperately tried to recall who it belonged to; somewhere hidden in her brain lay the image of its owner. Running along the corridors of her mind she stopped at every door to open them and peer in. Some were bolted shut from the inside, others swung open easily, revealing dark, empty rooms containing no answers.

Her quest was interrupted when the actual door to her hospital room opened and another person entered; the lady who walked in started to address the already present entity.

"Good Morning, Doctor."

"Mum!" Sophie yelled out from within a dark passageway. She started to track back along her route, breaking into a run and shouting as she went.

"Mum! I'm in here!" her voice echoed around the labyrinth of her mind. There was no response from outside her body; she continued until she reached the entrance but still there was no reaction from mum. Sophie paused.

"...still can't hear me..." said Sophie, sounding distraught. For the first time she felt broken; normally life's challenges were taken stride by stride, but this was a step too far. She had invested heavily in the notion that an escape from `Stalag Luft` would translate into freedom from the vice-like grip of her coma, but it wasn't to be. She found a dark corner within her mind and using the angle of two cerebral walls to support her body slowly slid towards the floor, slumping down with her head in her hands. She began to cry but no tears flowed.

As she floundered in the depths of her reality the conversation between Doctor Strange and her mum permeated into her consciousness.

"Hi, how are you?" Strange asked while flicking through Sophie's notes. He was dressed in casual clothes, if anything looking slightly scruffy for a head surgeon. He saw Sophie's mum looking at his unorthodox attire.

"It's my day off, I just dropped by to pick up some paperwork and thought I would check in on Sophie." Mum thanked him with a smile.

"So, what have you been talking about today?" he asked, as she sat down on the edge of Sophie's bed.

"More history; World War Two." She pulled out a bundle of college notes from her bag and began to sort through them. Then she stopped, suddenly a feeling of doubt tinged with guilt had penetrated her usual steadfast outlook; she was troubled that her interaction wasn't having a positive effect anymore.

"I hope I'm getting through; you do think her mind is still active?" The doctor sensed that mum was looking for strong reassurance, so he replaced Sophie's file and folded his specs away in order to give her his full attention.

"The human brain is fascinating; we still don't fully understand how they function, but we do know each trauma affects different brains in separate ways - Sophie's will be processing this situation in a manner that's unique to her."

"How do you mean?" Mum asked.

"The theory is, our brains while under duress continue operating with their default traits and characteristics from the person's normal personality; probably with a little distortion here and there, but fundamentally, the same."

Sophie's mum took comfort from this, knowing Sophie had always been an easy-going person, full of spirit and a sense of humour that served her well; if the doctor's theory was right, she knew Sophie would be ok, maybe not physically but psychologically.

"Thank you - that makes sense." she said, now feeling a little calmer. "It's your day off, you should get going - back to that gardening you've been doing."

"Pardon?" said the doctor slightly perplexed by her deduction.

"You've got earth all over your shoes." Mum replied, nodding down towards the floor. Sophie had been half listening to their conversation while sobbing softly to herself, but the words just uttered by her mum made her stop and lift her head up - they seemed insignificant, but deeply resonated within her.

"Hang on, Strange was in my dream, helping dispose of the soil on the allotment." Her mind began to tick over quicker, looking for relevance and meaning. "Now, he's at my bedside with earth all over his shoes..." From the dark recess of her mind where she was slumped, suddenly she jumped up and ran into a lighter, brighter space.

"He *is* helping me!" Her positivity had been rejuvenated. "I'm getting out of here." The light that illuminated her head space, bounced off the bright surfaces and gave her back the sense of optimism that she had abandoned. Buoyed by this turn of events, Sophie recognised she had to keep positive no matter what twists and turns lay ahead.

Mum and the doctor continued to chat for a few minutes, mainly about gardening and other non-hospital related subjects, meanwhile Sophie half listened to their conversation while making a mental note of all the things she wanted to do after the constraints of her coma were lifted.

"Find another job, spend more time with my family, try to improve my guitar playing - settle down with my boyfriend..."

There was a gentle knock at the door and a third person entered her room. Sophie paused to find out who had popped by.

"Hi." said the voice.

"Jake! What are you doing here? I thought you were abroad?" Sophie's mum was obviously acquainted with the visitor.

"The job finished earlier than expected, so I thought I would fly back and catch up with how the patient is doing." Sophie's mum nodded towards the doctor.

"There's the man to ask; he is the head `head` consultant." The doctor smiled and stood up to address the gentleman.

"Well, she is showing signs of activity on the scans which is positive, so I'm convinced she can hear us." This news was met with visible sense of relief; the doctor continued. "Interaction with Sophie is very important at this stage; it helps to promote stimulus within her cortex..."

"To keep the wheels moving?' suggested the man, to show understanding.

"Exactly. The mind is like the engine of a car, it has to be maintained in order for it to work properly. Words, music, ideas are the brain's lubricant; like a motor, if you don't add oil, it seizes up." It was a clear analogy and made perfect sense to all in the room, Sophie included.

"Her mum has been reading college notes to Sophie, but if you can also talk to her about, well, anything really I'm sure it will help."

"Sure thing." Jake appeared to be very willing to help.

The doctor hesitated - he realised he didn't actually know who he was addressing.

"How do you know Sophie?"

"I'm so sorry, I didn't introduce you properly." Sophie's mum interjected. "This is Jake, although Sophie has always called him Knobby. He is her brother."

* * *

Chapter 8

Sophie *still* lay on her bed, but now all alone. Mum and brother had spent time by her side reminiscing about happier times which Sophie relished listening to - smiling and nodding in recognition to each anecdote. The family holidays in Devon, the Christmas when grandad got tipsy, Knobby trying to sweep the chimney with the cat on his fourth birthday. All good times before life became complicated.

Although enjoying recalling childhood memories, Knobby`s jet lag was kicking in, he excused himself and departed - satisfied his sister was in good hands. Not long after, and with a pending work interview to oversee, mum also slipped away after leaving a kiss on her daughter`s forehead. Sophie continued with the trips down memory lane - it made a nice change revisiting her own history rather than someone else's, and after a spell of turbulence in her mind, she lay still, content that all was going to be ok.

* * *

As well as images, facts and figures, being a musician Sophie`s mind was also crammed with melodies, inherently stored away for future recall - over the years an impressive back catalogue had developed. To pass time, tunes were excavated from deep within her memory and brought to the surface to be either whistled or hummed depending on whichever suited - however Sophie`s indisposition had corrupted her filling system. Data had become somewhat scrambled; melodies emerged from obtuse angles, sometimes starting half way through a phrase or even before the previous excerpt had finished. The Beatles turned into Duke Ellington which quickly morphed into Prokofiev.

"Hmmm, Prokofiev." Sophie thought. She knew his most recognised composition was always on TV, but couldn't recall its title and no amount of brain scratching was going to produce results. The information had been misfiled. To assist, a helpful orchestra struck up a performance of the piece from somewhere within the warren that formed Sophie's mind, but this only added to her frustration.

"I know how it goes, thank you!" she shouted down the corridor at the obliging ensemble. Staring at a spot on the ceiling and clicking her fingers didn't help, so she joined in - humming along with the melody to help jog her memory. The weighty trombones punched out the lower end motif while the strident string section majestically carved out the melody above; it was a stirring piece of music which moved Sophie to sit up and begin to conduct the unseen orchestra.

"Got it! Romeo and Juliet!" She suddenly cried out, as the knot in her brain untied itself. The volume of the orchestra began to rise with the drama of the music and this in turn enthused Sophie to swing her legs off the bed and slowly march across the hospital bedroom. For a third time she was compelled to get up from her bed and walk.

Suddenly, she stopped.

"Hang on..." Doubt had started to creep in. "Is this the right thing to do?" she voiced out loud as fuzzy logic began to impede her thoughts.

"What if they've been trying to take my vitals every time I've been gadding about? The readings would come back without results... 'cos I'm not here!"

This began to play on Sophie's mind; the rationale was sound on certain levels, but completely bonkers on others. She was torn between remaining in bed to see what medical science could do or visit another, exciting historical setting where who knows what could happen.

Momentarily, Sophie hovered between two worlds, as if between this life and the next - the subsequent decision taken could significantly alter the consequence of her future. She sat back down on the bed and thought.

Her mind was blank to begin, not really knowing how to start to compute this scenario. She looked around for inspiration and saw the old mirror hanging on the wall. This had been the starting point for her journeys that had made her laugh, cry, cringe, get angry, worry about stuff, but above all - think. Sophie realised - experiencing this wide spectrum of emotions was proof she was still alive which in turn provided her with an overwhelming sense of optimism. Keeping her mind active was imperative for survival - if she were to simply curl up in bed it would be nothing short of a surrender to the dark forces that empowered her coma and she was not prepared to let that happen.

"You're never going to win!" Her cry echoed throughout the cavernous void within her mind. She stood up with determination, the orchestra was still playing but now sounded more pompous and resolute than ever - every note driving Sophie onwards as she strode purposefully up to the wooden framed mirror, curious to gain an insight into what her next historical character could be.

Sophie burst into laughter - nothing surprised her anymore. She faced the reflection of a well-healed Victorian gentleman, complete with an impressive handle-bar moustache that filled the mirror.

The music swelled even further, making her feel proud and for some reason, very business-like. The door was only a few paces away, the same door that she had twice left the safety of her life support machine to go through and twice found herself in separate dimensions on adventures that were bizarre and inexplicable - she had relished every moment! These exploits had taken Sophie back to modern day reality, albeit for brief interludes, but had afforded her glimpses of normal life; maybe this time a visit to the studios would result in her remaining there? She was ready to find out.

Straightening her tie and smoothing down a heavily waxed crop of hair, she made her way to the door, opened it and walked through.

The room she entered was situated on the first floor of a large townhouse and was ornate in style; wood panelled walls adorned with thick heavy-set paintings that wouldn't look out of place in an art gallery, stretched out before her. Through the open window the sounds of a bustling city street wafted in, along with a hazy, bright sunshine that lit up the dust as it floated around the room. Sophie focused on her surroundings to figure out where and when she was. Hawkers could be heard from the street below, bellowing incomprehensible gibberish but with a distinct cockney twang and mixed in was the sound of hooves trotting rhythmically over cobbled streets.

"London?" Sophie said to herself. Right on cue and close by, the unmistakable tones from the bell tower of Westminster Abbey rang out.

"Well that's that question answered. But, who am I?"

Immediately in front of her was an immense wooden table, covering several acres, (by Sophie's estimation), and was large enough to sit an entire board of company directors around - on the side that she stood, three chairs had been placed at the midway point. Opposite, there sat six chairs split evenly into two groups, and beyond them an open door through which Sophie could see a reception area. The table was bare apart from a black leather bound folder, embossed with the initials `MBW` and a couple of folded newspapers that appeared to be purposely placed in front of the middle chair.

Sophie mused at the surroundings, and taking in all the evidence tried to grasp some meaning behind it all, but she remained clueless. Hoping the newspapers that lay before her could help, she gathered them up and tilted the print towards the light. Both papers ran the same story but with differing styles of headline. The broadsheet went with: `The Great Stink- London's sewers overflow` while the red-top read `Westminster- Full of S...` A torn corner had obscured the rest of the title, but Sophie had seen enough.

Then it hit her.

"What the hell is that smell!" She hadn't noticed it before, but as well as sound and light originating from the street below, now another sense was being assaulted. Her nose detected a most horrid stench which could only be emanating from the drains. And the situation wasn't being helped by the hot, summer sun. Slumping down in the chair and almost overcome by the reeking aroma, her eyes began to smart, so she dabbed them with the sleeve of her white, cotton shirt.

As she sat there wondering what to do next, her bleary eyes became fixed on the posh folder that lay within reach. A few sheets of paper protruded from one corner as if to tempt her into reading them.

The first page was blank, except for a coat of arms emblazoned with a Latin script - the next however, revealed more. The minuets of a meeting held by the Metropolitan Board of Works in which permission was granted to engage, Sir Joseph Bazalgette to "...oversee the design and construction of the new London sewage system."

Sophie sat back in her chair.

"That's it, I must be Sir Joe." Her ponderings of this revelation were brief as two voices approached from the other room; a male and female were discussing the forthcoming selection process of candidates to be involved with this project, and they were heading straight for the boardroom. Before they entered, Sophie had instantly recognized them and wasn't the least bit shocked to see Doctor Strange stroll through the boardroom door - closely followed by her mum. Both were suitably dressed in period costumes and carrying clip boards under their arms. Sophie smiled and nodded to each as they made their way round the ridiculously large table to reach their respective seats; finally they sat down either side of the boss. Sophie's mum was the first to speak over the strains of Prokofiev.

"Orchestra rehearsing again, then?"

The doctor, who was busy making notes answered without looking up from his clip board.

"These offices have very thin walls."

"I wouldn't mind but they play the same bloody tune week in, week out." Sophie blurted out the first thing that came to mind, but both parties weren't really listening as they had become engrossed in preparing for what lay ahead. Thinking that she should also get ready for whatever it was that would occur next, Sophie shuffled her chair forward and straightened her back to adopt a more formal posture. As she did, her knee banged into something metal under the table; she frowned and peered down to find out what it was. Hanging from a hook was a small, brass funnel attached to what looked like a long hose pipe. Curious as to where it went, Sophie`s eyes followed the line of the pipe until is disappeared under the floorboards.

"Where the hell does that go?" she said to herself, noticing across the other side of the room the pipe re-immerged from the floor. It followed the vertical line of the wall, vanished through a hole which she assumed led into the reception room.

Suddenly, without warning the Doctor thumped his board down on the table.

"Sir! Shall we get things started?"

Sophie jumped and hurriedly emerged from the depths, intuitively grabbing the funnel as she passed it – luckily enough slack in the hose meant it could reach beyond the table top.

"Send in the candidates, please."

She issued her first instruction as Bazalgette by speaking down the brass cone, having worked out it was a crude intercom system. Her voice reverberated down the pipe and a faint echo could be heard as it reached the other end. A voice quickly returned back down the pipe.

"Yes, Sir Joseph."

* * *

It took a moment, but eventually the door opened and two - very different groups of people entered the board-room and peeled off into their respective teams, taking up positions opposite the panel. To Sophie`s left were three, obvious working class gentlemen – their clichéd apparel gave away the nature of each mans` occupation; a barrow boy, a blacksmith and a sweep, while their slovenly conduct indicated a total lack of social etiquette. Sophie was amused by this, but then looked beyond the exaggerated caricatures before her and realized that the trio were in fact Bob, Knobby and Johnson.

"Of course - who else?" She smiled inwardly.

The other group to her right were polar opposites and looked like the poshest collection of refined Victorian stereotypes her imagination could muster; the men were adorned by finery normal money could not buy. Sophie considered them, but didn't have a clue as to which part of her memory they had been dug up from. For all she knew, they were random strangers conjured from nowhere.

"Good morning!" she said abruptly, trying to get things moving; both teams came to attention and as one, mumbled back at her like a class of reception kids.

"Good morning, Sir Joseph."

Sophie set the scene, recalling details from an old essay she once wrote.

"As you know London has been blighted by an enormous build-up of raw sewage and the stench that prevails is unbearable..." she paused to gather more thoughts but before she could carry on, the head `Toff` butted in with a personal anecdote. His voice was one of the plumiest Sophie had ever heard and obviously he liked the sound of it.

"I had an audience with the Queen yesterday; she has taken to wearing a scented flamingo round her neck to mask the smell." he said - stretching every vowel to breaking point. Sophie was a little taken back, but soldiered on.

"Well, quite; so..."

At this point the second `Toff`, who clearly didn't want to be upstaged by the first, disregarded Sophie and added his own narration to the saga.

"I noticed the smell during high tea with Prince Albert; thought it was the pickled swan and sauerkraut - but his footman explained the drains aren't coping with the waste of the working classes." He looked down the table disdainfully at Bob's group and sneered. "Just like this lot."

All three bristled at the unnecessary torment and Bob being project manager felt obliged to defend them.

"Do you mind? I'm fed up with..." His protest was cut short by the first Toff who, ignoring Bob, spoke over him in a loud and commanding manner.

"I understand that Parliament may be suspended next week due to the smell emanating from the Thames..."

"No politicians! Ha! That should halve the amount of crap straight away." Johnson was quick off the mark; all the sparring with Bob over the years had sharpened his mind and he dealt the snobs a decisive - verbal right hand jab.

Sophie, however was still annoyed at being interrupted and took control of the situation by calling for some order.

"Gentlemen, please! I, Sir Joseph Bazalgette have been charged by the Metropolitan Board of Works to come up with a plan to alleviate London of this great stink, and I am seeking an apprentice."

The room fell silent as everyone's focus came back to the actual point of them being there. She continued.

"Now, I see you have organized yourselves into teams based on...annual salaries. What have you called yourselves?"

Although the question was directed at Bob the leader of the posh team spoke before he could answer.

"We have been motivated by the work of our colleague, Faraday; his research and development into the functionality of electricity has compelled us to name our team, `Dynamos`."

Sophie brushed aside his revelation with a simple `Ok`, and turned back to Bob.

"And your team name?"

"Tarmac!"

Sophie awaited an explanation for this odd name but it didn't arrive.

"Inspired by your travels down life's long and winding road?" she ventured, trying to add some gravitas to his ramblings - alas she was wasting her time.

"Nope, it was the first thing that came into my head."

Sophie felt aligned with team Tarmac; her brother was on board and although her boss was grumpy, she had known him a long time. Determined to make Bob look good in front of the Eton-elites, she decided to give his mediocre effort her blessing.

"I like that, it's spontaneous; you remind me, of me when I was starting out."

Bob was relieved; he liked the praise so with his new found confidence, decided to push his luck.

"Does this mean I get the job?" he asked.

"Crikey no, you have to undertake weeks of pointless tasks first."

"Like what?" Johnson piped up.

Sophie scrabbled through her imagination to find a suitable job for them to embark on; finally she stumbled upon the answer.

"First, each team will be given three baskets of fruit and veg. You must take them to the local market and sell the lot to make me a huge profit."

"I just came from the bleedin' market." Bob protested. "Gave up my stall to do this nonsense."

Sophie was on a roll and wasn't going to let anyone interrupt her.

"When you return, I will count the money and on the loosing team one of you will be shot." She wasn't sure if that last bit was right, but she figured it didn't really matter.

"Right! Be back here by five o'clock." she demanded.

Bob glared at Sophie and with a hint of frustration in his voice, he replied.

"No! *You* need to be back here by five o'clock..."

This was perplexing; why would a candidate talk to a prospective employer in this tone?

"I beg your pardon young man." she said trying her best to sound like a school matron, but Bob was unrepentant and continued with his rebuke.

"... have you not been listening to ...."

* * *

Sophie didn't know it but her dreamscape was about to dramatically change; Bob continued to speak his piece and nothing of significance interrupted it, however his voice was the only constant. In the space between two random words Sophie's mind leapt from the Victorian boardroom and flung Bob and herself back to the reception area of the studios – the others remained in the past. Bob didn't flinch, he simply carried on talking - his speech provided the only link with the previous scene.

"....a word I've been saying?" he concluded.

Sophie ignored the question; her mind feverishly trying to re-adjust itself from the vigorous shift in time and location. The rant continued, but her ears blocked out the noise as the knot in her muddled mind began to unravel. She thought the toggling back and forth between her imaginings was starting to make sense, but the switches in scenes had never occurred this abruptly.

Bob paused and waited for a response; Sophie continued to look vacant.

"Can you be back at the studio by five?" he repeated. Sophie`s mind slowly started to re-engage with reality.

"Sorry, I was miles away. What's happening?"

"For crying out loud, Soph!" Clearly frustrated by her lack of attention, Bob raised his voice and slowed down the syllables in order to clarify his remarks.

"Can you and the band be back here by five tonight?"

Sophie thought for a moment, then finally uttered a lucid and coherent answer.

"Not a chance!" She snapped.

"Why not?" he demanded, indignantly.

Sophie sensed `one of those` conversations brewing.

"Due to musical differences which were contrapuntal to the main ideal of the group, two of them have buggered off."

"To do what?"

Sophie tried to remain diplomatic.

"Move in new directions."

"What directions?" he demanded.

Realizing that diplomacy was probably a waste of time, Sophie now opted for a more honest approach.

"As far as possible and in the opposite direction to the manager."

"Hang on, that's me! Did they not like my style of management?"

"Nope!"

Sophie delivered her one word answer without a pause and like a wrecking ball crashing through an old brick wall, Bob`s confidence was shattered in one decisive strike.

"But..." initially he faltered while trying to find some meaningful words - finally he cobbled some thoughts together. "I thought you wanted to be a self-governing collective, with me just arranging the odd gig?"

"All your gigs were odd." came the obvious, curt reply.

"What do you mean?"

Somehow Bob had stirred up a latent emotion - as he looked quizzically expecting some qualification on the last comment, the gears in Sophie's mind turned in readiness for an argument. Like a barrister attending court, details were checked, speeches written, and evidence prepared, all in the blink of an eye. Then the prosecuting councillor took to the stand.

"Do you recall taking a booking for the twenty-first of June last year?"

"Err, hang on." The defendant screwed up his eyes tightly to aid recollection. "Got it!" Bob's eyelids bounced open which in turn forced his eyebrows upwards creating a facial expression as if to say: `Ta Da!` "The local bingo hall!" He felt smug having answered the question and added further detail for good measure. "Nine o'clock start, if I remember correctly."

Sophie was not impressed.

"How could we forget?" she quizzed. "You totally failed to mention it was nine in the morning."

The defendant went to interrupt with his version of events, but the prosecuting council hadn't finished.

"Who the hell books a band for that time of day?"

Bob's mouth opened and closed but no words formed; he looked like a guppy fish who had joined a choir but didn't know any of the words. The grilling continued.

"...you only bothered to phone us at eight-am to clarify the start time - one hours' notice!"

"In my defence, the band were all up and about anyway." Bob responded - it was a weak retort - factually correct but a complete dead end for this particular argument. Sophie snapped back at him without hesitating.

"Of course we were up and about - we hadn't even been to bed, no thanks to you." Although many months had passed she was still annoyed about this fact.

Now realising his line of defence was like watching a recently opened can of worms lose its contents, Bob began to shrink down into his shoulders. The reason why the entire band were available at that unorthodox hour filtered back into his consciousness.

"Oh yes. You were traveling back from that summer solstice gig at Stonehenge." came the meek reaction. Sophie become further agitated.

"Another of your zany gigs; a swing band at a Hippy convention!"

Bob went quiet. Sophie shouted.

"We stood out like an elephant farting in a duck pond."

He truly believed he had been trying his best to help Sophie; granted the gigs were slightly on the eccentric side, but work was work.

"You must have had some good gigs?" he said, feeling subdued and slightly numb.

"Can't think of any." was Sophie's brusque reply.

There was a lull in proceedings during which Bob awkwardly shuffled some papers around while pulling several facial contortions as he contemplated what to say next. Keen to keep Sophie on side as her help was needed, Bob needed to find a way to express how much energy he had exerted to push the band forward – all without reward, but avoiding further confrontation. It was a lonely walk across that particular tightrope, but one he had made on many occasion. Breaking the silence, he finally plucked up the courage to attempt to gain some mediocre recognition for his hard graft.

"What about that support slot I booked for you?" Momentarily Bob thought he was on the high ground as a vision of a successful evening filled his mind. "Remember? You opened for that experimental art-house band..." Bob stumbled and a fair amount of finger clicking followed. "...what were they called?"

Sophie knew exactly which gig Bob was referring to; it had been a specific low-light from her playing career. She looked at him and almost sighed the answer.

"They called themselves `Gig Cancelled`."

"That was it!" Bob said excitedly. His recollection was the night had been a roaring success; he just needed to hear this from Sophie. "And, how did that go?" he asked expectantly.

Sophie slammed her paperwork down on the desk and glared; Bob instinctively knew her next sentence probably wasn't going to be as positive as he had hoped.

"Do I need to explain? No bugger turned up - the main act didn't even bother putting in an appearance."

Bob, not for the first time in his life was feeling bewildered, knowing that it didn't really matter what he said next - much like Al Capone's defence lawyer, his closing speech was purely for the record and would have no impact on the summing up. He was going down.

"I don't understand. – what was the point of that?"

"It was a social experiment - they wanted to see which section of society would buy a ticket to see a band with that name."

"What did they find out?"

"Nobody's that stupid, the whole thing was a colossal waste of time." Sophie's tough stance didn't let up. "Honestly, the cat has better administration skills than you."

This doubly annoyed Bob - nothing he did for them seemed good enough and it appeared the cat was trying to muscle in on his job. He rose up from his seat and spoke at a level just under a shout.

"Bloody charming!" he said, finding his belligerent voice. "Do you know how difficult you lot are to manage?" Sophie began to wonder if she had pushed Bob too far as he continued to sound off. "One needs the negotiation skills of a diplomat, the two faces of a politician, and three pairs of eyes to constantly watch where to tread."

"What do you mean by that?" said Sophie, now being forced to defend herself.

"Basically, the band has more egg shells lying around than an omelette factory."

"Utter rubbish!"

Silence - There was brief adjournment while they both revised their points of view.

"Ok. Look, I'm sorry." Bob let his apology permeate through the atmosphere before carrying on. "I try my best for you; sometimes I get it wrong..." The stiffness in his voice subsided; he knew a softer approach was required and sooner rather than later the conversation had to turn around as he needed

Sophie's assistance. Bob let the tainted atmosphere dissipate for a few more seconds before one last effort to dispel the myth of his ineptitude.

"I was going to bring this up later, but I've just had a call from a top agent offering a very prestigious gig."

Sophie suddenly felt terrible; she recognized Bob did work hard, albeit very inefficiently, but the voice in her head was currently telling her to take it easy on him. She began to back-pedal and mellowed her approach accordingly, while her imagination began to turn over with all the possibilities of what Bob's posh gig could be.

"High profile? That sounds interesting. What is it?"

Bob didn't answer the question immediately, but instead skirted round the subject, merely volunteering marginal information.

"It involves an all-expenses paid trip over water."

He hesitate, ensuring Sophie had absorbed this little nugget – she had and was now picturing herself on board a ocean liner, sailing in exotic waters into a clichéd sunset.

"Interested?" he added, feeling genuinely excited to be imparting these facts. After their recent disagreements, he sincerely believed this olive branch would help reconcile their differences.

"Wow! Yes. Definitely" She struggled to find the right words. "I'm so sorry; I got a bit emotional earlier." She let her apology hang long enough so Bob would know that it was genuine, but not so long that it delayed the big reveal of the mystery engagement.

"So, what's the gig? A cruise ship round the Med?" she asked expectantly.

"No - the Woolwich ferry needs a band for a promotion they are running." said Bob in a very matter-of-fact way.

Sophie didn't quite know how to react, but the vacant expression now displayed across her face spoke volumes; Bob studied the reaction carefully before concluding that, probably this wasn't the big hit he thought it would be. After a short period of contemplation from Sophie, she decided to write off the last few minutes of her life and move on.

"So, what's happening at five?"

It took Bob a couple of beats to realize Sophie was referring back to their opening chat, and after the preceding events he really didn't expect any interest from his next request, so he delivered it in a dismissive tone.

"Oh, that - I've got the local news coming in to film here in the studios; I was going to have you lot playing."

Sophie looked up; she was inquisitive.

"Why are they filming here?"

"I persuaded them to do a promotion for us." Bob`s answer had an air of ambiguity which Sophie intuitively detected.

"Local news teams don't do promos, they cover things like the opening of a new public convenience." Sophie, as per usual had begun to unravel Bob`s yarn and he started to back track.

"Well, it's not strictly a promo for us..." Bob paused, deluded that enough information had been imparted and the topic of conversation could move on, but all it took was a glare from Sophie accompanied by one raised eyebrow and he buckled.

"I think they may be under the impression that we are holding a fundraising event."

"Why on earth would they think that?"

"'Cos, that's what I told them." said Bob, but this wasn't enough; Sophie wanted full disclosure.

"What exactly did you say?"

"I said, we are holding a fundraising event." Bob averted his eyes.

"For what are we supposed to be raising money for?"

"To get the sewers moved." Bob was still being slightly evasive. Clearly this wasn't the complete story and Sophie being tenacious by nature was not going to let it end there.

"What?" she snapped.

"Err, they want to build this thing..." Bob continued to waffle. "...but the drains are in the way so I'm raising money to have them altered."

"What thing?" said Sophie getting very frustrated. Bob knew from her body language it was time to come clean.

"A donkey sanctuary."

"What's the bloody point of that? Why would people give money to move the sewers by three foot so Eeyore can get a retirement home?"

"I made it up." Bob held his head in shame and spoke with a submissive tone; his intentions had been honourable - the profile of the studio needed to be raised - somehow bookings and therefore turnover were slipping. Bob couldn't work out why this was; Sophie knew - a key member of staff had been hospitalised and the remaining operative was a dullard. However, she sensed that he needed supporting and, long term it would benefit her. She pondered for a moment.

"Well, I suppose if the TV bods are happy to cover the event, it could be a bit of fun."

After the recent fractious conversation, Bob was taken aback by Sophie's sudden warming to his idea, and although he was lifted by this there was a slight flaw in the plan.

"It would be fun, but we don't have a band."

"I'm sure we could cobble something together; I could play bass." Sophie was keen to have a bit of TV exposure and wasn't ready to let the notion die just yet. Bob scratched his head and thought carefully through all the possibilities.

"Perhaps Knobby and Johnson could step in on drums and lead guitar ?"

"I didn't think you liked Johnson." Sophie queried. "You said he was a feckless wonder."

"That's not quite what I said." muttered Bob.

"Thinking about it they are booked in for tonight anyway; we just have to ask them to get in a bit earlier."

Bob started to see a way through; he stood up and searched for a scrap piece of paper to make notes.

"Right." he said, pen poised. "Lead vocals?"

"No problem." Sophie sounded confident. "I'll give my mate Nick a ring, I'm sure he would be up for it."

Then an idea struck Sophie that she thought would be the icing on the cake.

"Hey, we should get a horn section in; have them jigging around at the back. It would look great for the cameras."

"I can't pay them!" Bob`s reflex reaction kicked, almost before Sophie had finished talking.

"Don't worry, I think Nick knows some local session guys who will probably just do it for a laugh."

"Great! They do they know what they're doing?"

Sophie realized Bob wasn't quite comfortable with this, so she sought to dispel any fears he had.

"No worries; back in the day they were always on Top of the Pops."

"Fantastic. Can you ask him to sort it?"

"Will do." Sophie picked up her phone and began to scroll down her contacts to make the initial call; then a wry smile crept across her face. She looked up at Bob who was busy scribbling more notes.

"So what are you going to do?"

He stopped writing and looked up.

"What do you mean?"

Sophie had an idea that she thought would be positive for Bob, the studio and even their relationship.

"I think it would be great to have you in the band as well."

"But I don't play anything."

"That doesn't matter, just stand at the back with the horn section and mime along with the pro`s."

For a split second, Bob liked the idea but doubt started to creep in.

"I'm not sure I could do that."

"Come on, what could go wrong? It'll be fun!" Sophie said to encourage him; she could see he was seriously thinking about it.

"Maybe..."

"Listen, all you have to do is keep an eye on the others; when they play, just mimic what they do." she said to reassure him. "Don't worry, the cameras don't ever stay on one shot for very long."

She sensed he was wavering, so the cajoling continued. "My mum still has my brother's trumpet in the loft, you could use that." Bob dithered some more, so Sophie beamed a huge smile of encouragement.

"Go on!" she said.

"Oh, all right, I'll give it a go. Actually I've always fancied being on TV."

Sophie felt an enormous sense of accomplishment, trying to get Bob to do anything that didn't form part of his normal routine was a mission, but this time she had surpassed herself; he appeared genuinely pleased to have been asked and almost relieved to be involved with something outside his mediocre, predictable existence.

"Thanks Soph; I'm sure it will be fine." Bob smiled back at Sophie. "Like you say, what on earth could go wrong...?"

* * *

Suddenly, her warm glow of satisfaction generated by the rare connection with Bob went cold and it's radiance dimmed. She blinked; just once, but within that wafer thin, fleeting moment of her timeline, Sophie and Bob was instantaneously transported back to Victorian London finding herself seated around the outsized boardroom table and taking on the image of Bazalgette once more.

"What the hell is going on?" Sophie thought, bewildered as to why her travels had suddenly become disjointed; even within the context of her current medical predicament, this most recent dream was on track to be the most surreal experience as yet encountered.

* * *

Chapter 9

Nothing had changed in the dusty, smelly board room, Sophie's mum still sat to her right, Dr. Strange on her left, both busy making notes; the two groups of candidates opposite had begun to squabble among themselves over workers' rights or some other nonsense, Sophie wasn't really paying attention. Suddenly her nasal passages were assaulted by a foul stench that infused the area - much like smelling salts that rudely interrupt a slumbering patient, her mind was brought into sharp focus. Shaking her head as if trying to avoid each and every pungent particle and with smarting eyes, she looked around at the others; they didn't appear to be bothered by it. Maybe they had grown accustomed, but having just arrived from the relatively odour free studio, in a split second the ambient fragrance had gone from 'musty musician' to an overwhelming whiff of the capital's woeful lack of sewage management. Sophie looked over at her brother sitting nearest the window; he was extoling the virtues of the National Union of Chimney Sweeps.

"...and another thing; at the last quarterly meeting it was ratified that the hourly rate for weddings should rise in line with inflation, and the act of sweeping chimneys, stacks, conduits etc. should not hinder the engagement of our members by happy couples to attend said weddings..."

"Knobby!" Sophie shouted across the table.

"The wind has changed direction, shut the window please."

The conversation within the room fell silent and Knobby, who was slightly annoyed at being interrupted mid flow, stood up and shuffled towards the source of the smell, muttering loudly enough so Sophie could hear.

"I wondered when I was going to get a part in this daydream."

Johnson, while looking in Sophie's direction, spoke out of the side of his mouth in support of his colleague.

"Don't worry, I've only had a couple of lines so far."

"That's two more than me, Lovie." Bellowed the Toff on the extreme right as he leant over the table to converse with Johnson at the far end.

"Silence!" demanded Sophie, annoyed at the passive mutiny of her imagination, but the Toff continued to dribble on to his colleagues. Enough was enough, Sophie rose to her feet to address him directly.

"Stop this! I don't even know who you are."

He broke off talking to the snobs.

"Well, I must be in your subconscious memory somewhere." said the indignant fop. Feeling like the director of a local am-dram society dealing with disgruntled bit-part actors, this insubordination irritated Sophie, but there was an underlying emotion that bothered her more. She felt uncomfortable by the contextual ambiguity of the last conversation; un-written rules had been disobeyed - the fourth wall had been broken, not by her, but others who really shouldn't be in a position to do this. Her dream – her rules!

Maybe it was a sign; perhaps outside influences were infiltrating her subconscious?

* * *

The heavy sash window slid down with a thud and for a moment there was relief from the pungent battering the collective noses had endured; the groups mumbled among themselves which gave Sophie time to think. Up until the recent twisting of her logic, she had been content to busk her way through the various situations, now she was unsure how to handle this new dimension. The conversations around her grew as heated debates broke out about the Great Stink and what could be done.

Sophie sat back down and purposefully smacked the desk with open palms to bring attention back to her; she realised the best and only way forward was to bring proceedings back into line and continue with her fantasy.

"Right you lot!" The room fell silent. "I want to hear from each leader your team's ideas on how to tackle the problem. Dynamo, you first."

The head aristocratic ass puffed himself up, straightened his spectacles and stood up to speak.

"First, we thought a law could be passed making it illegal for the working classes to perform any bodily functions between Monday and Friday..." Immediately there were murmurs of protest from along the table which he duly ignored and raising his finger to command the floor, he carried on. "...but on reflection, we thought that's just not on."

He paused to take a sip of water from the cut glass crystal tumbler before him leaving a gap in the conversation. Bob piped up.

"Finally! A consideration for the lower classes. Politicians always dump on us from..."

"No, you misunderstand." He was cut off mid-sentence by the condescending Toff. "It's because we wouldn't make any money."

His associates made peculiar grunting noises and shuffled their papers to show their admiration and support, all of which the Toff lapped up like a potty trained toddler being praised by cooing parents. He continued.

"My colleagues and I propose to pass a motion stating that anyone wanting to pass a motion during the working week, would need to pay a levy."

He sat down to a rapturous round of congratulatory back slapping for a fine presentation. Sophie didn't like it, she always thought politicians were only in the job for self-gain and this proved it. She wanted to drop them down a couple of pegs.

"But what if poorer citizens can't afford to pay? They would become bunged up."

"That's why it's called the Congestion Charge." He smirked. "However, we do have the needs of the lower class voters in mind; if someone had little money we would offer some assistance."

"How?" asked Sophie, she didn't trust them and with good reason.

"The right honourable gentlemen to my left has a financial interest in a cork factory. The poor could purchase...."

"Lease!" The right horrible gentleman on his left cut in to correct him.

"Sorry, lease a cork from us which could be inserted..."

"No-one is going to do that." interrupted Sophie. She was annoyed; apart from the obvious egotistical commercial aspect, the plan was fundamentally flawed. "By doing this you are only delaying the inevitable quagmire until the weekend."

"How do you mean?" The Toff looked concerned, had she seen a problem with their perfect plan.

"Well, instead of having a constant flow throughout the week, come the weekend a tsunami of poo would overwhelm the already over burden drains."

"'A poo-nami?' Bob piped up.

"Exactly." said Sophie. "This is not getting to the root of the problem."

"No it`s not, but it will make me rich!" The Toff finally showed his true colours, while the other two posh twits guffawed in a way that only rich Victorian gents knew how. Bob had heard enough.

"You lot are so full of what's flowing down Fleet Street. Isn't it obvious? We need a larger sewer."

Sophie was relieved that Bob had intervened and with an idea that actually made sense.

"At last, somebody with some intelligence."

"Does this mean I've got the job?" Bob repeated his cheeky question from earlier.

"Not a chance! You still have to produce some organic yogurt, and start a business manufacturing banjos. Tell me your idea on how to get a bigger sewer?"

Bob started to get very excitable, as if he had a show-stopping idea; turning to Knobby he gestured to get his attention.

"Pass me the map, son."

Knobby looked up from doing a crossword.

"Blimey, me again?" he said reaching down to collect a large tube which lay beside his feet. "Twice in the same dream!"

He unscrewed the cap and pulled out a large piece of rolled up parchment which he passed to Bob, who carefully unrolled the map and slid it across the table for the boss to examine. It was a very detailed, Victorian map of London with ornate italic writing and fine etchings around the margins which drew the eye. Sophie gazed intently at the map, trying to soak up as much of the detail as possible; she knew contemporary London very well, and could make out the large buildings and areas that were familiar to her - Waterloo and Kings Cross stations and such like, but what stood out in her mind were the landmarks that were absent; the iconic Tower Bridge was missing leaving conspicuous gaps on both sides of the Thames embankment, and in Kensington, a large open area to the south of Hyde park was lacking the Royal Albert Hall.

Sophie revelled in these snippets of historical facts and figures, but her concentration was soon interrupted by Bob who, to help with his presentation had produced a telescopic pointer and was currently waving it at the map from the other side of the table.

"So, Sir, as you can see, this is the line of the old sewer." Bob, unaware of his lack of control, enthusiastically thwacked the pointer down on the chart, narrowly missing Sophie`s knuckles. "What I propose is we re-route it here, here and here..." Each recommendation was accompanied by another thwack of the pointer. "...with a larger tunnel, and re-join the existing one, right over .... Here." Thwack! A definitive full stop to Bob`s strategy that must have left a dent in the table.

"I'm not sure about this area?" Sophie said, indicating to a small square off the Euston Road. "What if, one day someone wants to build a donkey sanctuary here?"

"Can't stand in the way of progress..." enthused Bob. "...and the beauty of this plan is, there already exists a wide-bore tunnel running along the northern part of the route; we could use that and save a fortune in tunnelling costs."

Sophie squinted at the map then looked up at Bob.

"That's the Metropolitan line; you can't use that!"

"Oh, crap. Really?" Bob`s face dropped and he looked quite despondent. Sophie didn't really want to shatter Bob`s dream, but ironically his vision for the new sewer system had just gone down the old one; looking very forlorn, he stood up and left the room.

Sophie felt responsible for hurting his feelings, so she quickly followed him, having first negotiated her way round acres of table. Upon reaching the boardroom door that Bob had slammed on his way out, she could hear him on the other side talking in a raised voice. Grasping the brass handle she opened the door and stepped through. As her foot landed in the next room, immediately her situation instantaneously morphed - she was back in the reception area of the studios with all its modern day trappings and suitably dressed for the period.

* * *

Sophie blinked a few times, her mind readjusting to its altered surroundings; she could hear the muffled sounds of bands practicing in distant rooms and musicians loitering around the lobby eating crisps and talking nonsense. Bob paced around while conversing with a voice on the end of a phone; it sounded to Sophie that the caller was berating him; his side of the dialogue was very apologetic.

"Oh crap, really?"

To Sophie's surprise Bob repeated his last sentence uttered in the boardroom, almost as if the conversation from the past had moved seamlessly into the future so not to disrupt any continuity.

"So sorry, dear..." Sophie promptly realized Mrs. Marsh was the other voice; the telephonic rebuke continued. "Ok dear..... Yes, dear. Bye." Bob returned the phone to its cradle and looked at Sophie. "Well, it's official. I'm in the dog house, and the dinners in the cat."

"What have you done now?" asked Sophie focussing her strong gaze on Bob in the same way an interrogator would focus a strong light in the face of a spy; of the two, Sophie's was far more intense and effective.

"I forgot to pick her up this morning."

"From where?"

"Hospital." confided Bob - the truth began to be revealed.

"What was she doing there?"

"Visiting someone..." Bob paused. "...And she had an operation on her foot." Sophie didn't say anything, she didn't need to, the death ray stare burned into Bob's conscience, testing his integrity.

"It was a very minor operation." He quickly added.

"And you didn't feel you should have been there to collect her?" Sophie enquired. Bob knew he was a marked man.

"It's not that far to walk...." he swallowed hard. "...and the rain had eased off a bit by then." He knew this sounded very lame.

"Can I offer you some advice?" said Sophie, not that she waited for his answer. "A very large bouquet of flowers is required; further to this, whatever you thought you were going to spend on a bunch; triple it!"

"Eighteen quid!" he retorted.

* * *

Bob had never been so happy to see Knobby and Johnson - having just walked into the reception they offered him a much needed reprieve. With an audible sense of relief he called over to them.

"Ah, just the two people I need to see. What are you guys doing tonight?" he asked with an abnormal amount of gusto. Johnson looked at him suspiciously.

"We've got our usual room booked." He couldn't quite understand why he was asking, the duo had been using the studio on the same day, at the same time for years.

"Perfect!" exclaimed Bob. "We have the local news filming here later and my band are short of a drummer and guitarist. Any chance you could both be here at five to stand in?"

"I've got my parkour meeting at five." said Knobby, shaking his head.

"You got your what, meeting?" Bob asked, suddenly feeling very out of his depth.

"Don't you know what parkour is?"

"Course I do! Our dining room floor is covered with it."

"That's parquet." Sophie felt obligated to join in at this point. Knobby shot her a look as if to say, 'I've got this one...'

"Parkour is free running..." he said.

"Free?" Bob interjected. "Obviously nobody is going to pay to jog around here."

Sophie listened intently, curious how this conversation was going to play out; she could see the pair of them were on two diverging conversational paths, but never could have predicted that the discourse would, at any moment, lead to her spinning abruptly back to the Victorian board room.

Knobby took a beat to gather his thoughts before speaking; wondering if he should play the `generation` card, or keep it simple and just explain the facts. Opting for the later, he tried not to sound too condescending.

"No, you misunderstand; it's a modern way to keep fit. We plan a route between two points using the urban landscape."

"There's nothing new about that." Bob said with misplaced authority. "People have been doing it for decades."

"No, it started in France in the late eighties." Knobby couldn't quite understand where Bob was going with this; even more so with his next question.

"Have you not seen Mary Poppins?" He spoke as if it was a perfectly ordinary thing to ask. "Dick Van Dyke and that mob were bouncing around the rooftops of London years ago."

Sophie covered her face to hide her emotions- half awkwardness, half stifled mirth. Head in hands she wondered how Bob could get it so wrong and yet, logically on an esoteric level, so right? Sophie composed herself and raised her head from her palms.

* * *

Everything had changed - again; she was back sitting in the board room dressed in Victorian apparel; Bob's map still spread out in front of her, the candidates, Dr, Strange and her mum still sat around the table. Sophie was dumbfounded by the speed and frequency at which the recent changes in her backdrops were occurring – she stopped to consider the rationale behind it and asked herself some searching questions, but her concentration was suddenly shattered by an almighty racket coming from the roof. Footsteps clattered around - not randomly but with a certain rhythm; they were accompanied by loud cockney voices requesting that everyone step in time.

"Bloody chimney sweeps!" she shouted, looking upwards to address the source of the noise.

Sophie had suddenly become very irritated by this dreamscape; having talked herself into entering this particular world and being convinced it would lead to an escape from her coma, no progress was being made and if anything, the process was being frustrated by her nearest and dearest. If she was being honest with herself, the situation had taken a dramatic twist and now, feeling cornered, frightened almost, she lashed out.

"Knobby!" she screeched. "Have a word with your lot, will you?"

"Great, is that all I do in this daydream?" said the petulant sibling.

"What if I don't want to?" Knobby was indignant at his sisters tone.

"All right, I'll make it easy for you." Pulling rank, Sophie raised her right hand, extended her index finger and uttered two simple words.

"You're fired!"

Knobby didn't argue, he realised he had probably gone too far; he stood up slowly and magnanimously withdrew from the table thanking his sister for the opportunity. Sacking her brother didn't quell Sophie's frustrations; still riled she turned her focus on Bob.

"Tell me why I shouldn't fire you."

"Well, actually I'm *your* boss." Bob said succinctly.

"Not in this dream you're not." she volleyed back at him.

The leader of the Toffs sat back in his chair with a schadenfreude induced grin smeared across his face which Sophie noticed out the corner of her eye. Full of pent up anger and with the speed of a striking viper - but with a more venom, she verbally pounced on him.

"Right, you jumped up little turd, tell me why you should stay in this process."

For the first time, probably in his entire privileged life, the Toff was being challenged: he was in no way equipped to deal with the mounting pressure and spluttered his way through a reply.

"Err... well ... I've have some great ideas.... and, err ... always given you one hundred and ten percent." The Toff thought that was a reasonable phrase to use; shallow and non-committal, but enough to throw Sophie off the scent.

"How the hell have you managed to do that?" she forcefully enquired. The Toff stalled - that soundbite had always worked in the past.

"Well...err ...err..." He stumbled over his words and sounded like a two-stroke engine running out of petrol. No-one had ever asked him to qualify his maths before. "I worked to my full potential ...err ... then worked ten percent harder?"

"Rubbish! The human body has a finite capacity..." Sophie began to unravel the Toffs illogical statement. "...if, as you claim you were already working at maximum effort, by definition you have no room for extra productivity."

"Maybe it was one hundred and eight percent?" said the Toff, missing the point.

"Whatever you are using to measure this self-adjudication of your output - I suggest you get it recalibrated."

This well-crafted sentence, executed with precision left the exasperated Toff teetering on the brink stupidity – his only option for survival was to turn on his fellow team member.

"You should fire him." he said panicking, while pointing to the equally aristocratic twit to his left. "He came up with the silly idea of badger walking."

His upper-class colleague quickly turned into a frantic, Eton-mess.

"Wait, No; Err... well at least I didn't suggest we open a brothel in Whitechapel."

Dr. Strange, who up until this point had been quietly making notes, placed his pen down on the table and turned to talk directly to Sophie - causally he spoke in a calm voice.

"Hello."

It was a simple, passive word that had been delivered among several aggressive ones uttered in the previous melee; an oasis amid a spoken tempest, but it still confused Sophie enormously. Strange had been silent all this time and along with her mum, dutifully observing proceedings, but now he only just decided to greet her...

"Hello, what?" Sophie replied.

And that was that; yet again she was sent hurtling forward through history until, within the blink of an eye, she was back in the studio, her mind a beat behind the rest of her which only added to her haphazard perception.

* * *

Chapter 10

The scene that greeted Sophie was not what she expected; the reception area was bustling with an air of expectation as an outside broadcast team from the local television company were running cables, checking sound levels and adjusting lighting rigs. Looking around, she noticed Knobby and Johnson, both now in modern garb, setting up their equipment along with other band members. The whole area was a general commotion of industrious individuals working to make ready for transmission.

After scanning the room, Sophie's vision came back into line with the Doctor who was still standing in front of her, smiling placidly.

"Hello." He repeated his greeting. Sophie was muddled, she knew who he was in everyday life, but in this charade his persona was a total mystery; she took a very wild guess.

"Hi, nice to see you. Are you part of the horn section?" He didn't respond immediately, but when he did there was a degree of hesitation.

"Yes." He paused. "I could give that a go."

"Great! Nick said you chaps are a bit wacky; nice guy, isn't he." Sophie looked for a glimmer of recognition in the doctor's eyes, but he just smiled vacantly; she also had picked up on the lack of conviction in his answer. In normal circumstances this would have caused alarm, but given her recent frame of mind, she was prepared to let it go, accepting that anything could, and probably would happen. 'Life's too short' she thought.

"Nick is running late..." Sophie said to break the awkward silence. "Thought he would be here by now."

The doctor quickly adopted the conversational thread and added his own stilted, artificial response.

"So - he's not here yet - then."

Sophie was puzzled, clearly he didn't have a clue who Nick was. His conduct all along had been on the `strange` spectrum - it was why she had given him that moniker in the first place, but this was different. Maybe he was trying to reach out to her? - From beyond the limits of her own mind, on a level so cryptic not even the queen of random herself could figure it out. Sophie wasn't sure, but she was ready to react swiftly if it were the case. The doctor continued to speak.

"Bad timekeeping - not what you want from a drummer!" The doctor laughed at his own joke, however Sophie didn't – was he testing her?

"No; Nick is the singer." she corrected him.

"Yes, vocalist! Silly me." He paused to collect his thoughts, once they were gathered together he swept them aside and blabbed the first load of old nonsense that struck his thoughts. "Of course, he *was* also a drummer - once taught Ringo Starr's next door neighbour..." He froze, aborting the sentence having realized his rather ambitious, over-commitment to the topic. Hoping Sophie hadn't noticed, he tried hiding behind a wall of silence.

"To do what?" Sophie enquired, seeing right through his esoteric barricade.

"Not sure." came the very weak reply.

Sophie thought about pursuing a sensible answer, but she realised it was probably a waste of brain power, so she chose to let him off the hook. Taking everything at face value, Sophie moved the conversation on.

"Right, did Nick explain what the gig was all about?" She knew this was a pointless question.

"He was a bit sketchy." said the doc.

"No worries, just join the other lads at the back and cover the brass parts. Where's your horn?"

"At the cleaners." he replied.

Time was ticking and the TV crew were almost ready - pressure was mounting. Luckily while looking out a trumpet for Bob, she had found both her brother's main instrument and his spare, so she handed that to Strange.

"You can use this." He reluctantly took the old, battered-up trumpet and with the same degree of trepidation that someone would handle a flask of weapons grade plutonium, held it out at arm's length.

A smartly dressed man with perfectly coiffured hair, and a cheesy smile approached Sophie and offered out his hand for her to shake.

"Hi there, I'm Cliff Stiffman from the `Look Here` section of the news."

Sophie considered the clipped, well-heeled figure before her, obviously she recognized him from the T.V. but she felt they had met before. Suddenly, it hit her; he had been sat opposite her in the Victorian boardroom, third Toff on the left.

"That's where I know you from!" she exclaimed.

Her hasty outburst thrilled the anchor-man; he was always pleased to be recognized by a fan. He was about to engage with his admirer when Bob came crashing through the door and made his way towards the group - he was excited to meet the man off the telly, but more importantly, the studios were about to receive some much needed publicity. He bounded over, grabbed Stiffmans` hand shook it enthusiastically.

"Good evening, Clive; love your work." said Bob.

"It's Cliff, actually." Bob didn't hear, he was too busy cueing up his introduction.

"Sorry I'm late; Bob Marsh, owner of Caramel Two Studios, and organiser of this event."

"Pleased to meet you; I was just chatting to your band members." Stiffman nodded towards Strange which took Bob by surprise; he squinted at the doctor, then at Sophie as if to demand an explanation.

"Another mate of Nicks..." she blurted out to avoid any embarrassment. Luckily time was pressing - Stiffman looked at his watch and became slightly agitated.

"Right guys, we are due on air very soon; in the first section we will profile the band - probably ask a couple of you some questions – that sort of thing."

This alarmed Sophie, interaction with the wrong personnel, especially on live TV, could prove disastrous for all concerned. Worriedly, she looked over at the band busy preparing; Knobby was making last minute alterations to the angle of his ride cymbal, Johnson was tuning up his guitar; suddenly she had a bad feeling.

"What sort of questions?" she asked.

"Just a bit of background stuff; don't worry I'll keep it light." said Stiffman while a junior made last minute alterations to his make-up.

"Positions please." shouted a woman with a clip board and dungarees. Sophie hurriedly thrust the other trumpet into Bob`s hands and ushered him and Strange over to the professional horn players across the other side of the room; she was about to go and get ready when Stiffman piped up.

"Can I borrow you for some quick admin?" The lady with the dungarees handed him the clipboard and he began to read some questions from the page.

"Have you filled out the PRS form?"

"Yes, did that earlier." Sophie was nervous, they were going live in a few moments and her two `imposters` in the ranks were still figuring out which end of the trumpet to use, while Knobby was faffing around with his kit and Johnson was being frustrated by his out of tune guitar. Her heart started to beat faster as Stiffman spoke again.

"As this will be a live broadcast I have to ask; are any of your band members prone to swearing?"

"Err...No." she said.

"Bollocks!" said Johnson, with split second timing he had over-tuned his `E` string and it dramatically snapped with a metallic twang. Sophie had just managed to catch sight of this and being around musicians for years, knew this to be the default phrase uttered upon a mishap. With a well-timed cough she managed to cover up Johnson's indiscretion and Stiffman was none the wiser.

"Sorry to ask that question, but the station's protocol had to change following a festive broadcast we did from the local kids Borstal last December."

"Dare I ask what happened?" Sophie was inquisitive.

"Let's just say, their version of The Twelve Days of Christmas was not the original one – in fact the only line they got right was `five gold rings`, but put in the context of the first four days, it took on a whole different meaning."

Sophie had switched off: the pending band interview was playing on her mind and she wanted clarification on who was going to be selected; if the anchor chose Nick's mates, they wouldn't have a clue what to say, and God only knows what would happen if he engaged in conversation with either Bob or Strange. She shuddered at the thought.

"Just a quick thought re: the interviews ....." she was interrupted when Stiffman's mobile rang.

"Sorry, it's the producer; I need to get this." He broke off listening to her to take the call from someone called Pippa.

Sophie carried on attempting to communicate with the pre-occupied Stiffman, but it was a challenge.

"Don't talk to the guys at the back, they're just making the numbers up." Along with plenty of exaggerated gestures, she half mouthed, half spoke, endeavouring to convey her message. Repeating this twice, eventually she caught his eye, but Stiffman just smiled inanely and gave a feeble 'thumbs up'. He walked away from away from Sophie, and began to wind up his call.

"Are you getting the line-feed back at base? Excellent! Talk to you in a few minutes. OK. Bye."

The call ended and he glanced up from his phone; everyone was looking at him expectantly.

"Right folks, we're on right after the 'missing ladder' feature." He returned his phone to his jacket pocket and handed the clipboard to a passing assistant. "Think, I'll go for a quick pee before they move the drains." he muttered.

Sophie watched the newsman stroll down the corridor and suddenly become quite nervous; the atmosphere was charged with anticipation; Nick had just turned up so this was one less thing to worry about, but she was still concerned about the horn players. She sidled up to the singer and greeted him with a friendly hug.

"Hey Nick, Nice to see you; thanks for turning up!"

Nick was one of those guys who was always took things in their stride; un-flustered and cool, Sophie needed someone like this round her at the moment to help keep her feet on the ground.

"Hey, no problem; wouldn't miss this for the world."

"Thanks for sorting out the `horn` guys - they will be ok, won't they? No rehearsal and all that."

"Yeh, no worries." Nick could see Sophie was troubled and tried to reassure her. "Those boys were always booked for TV work; not the live stuff mind, but back in the day you couldn't switch on the box without seeing them jigging around behind Kylie or George Michael."

That was good enough for Sophie, she went to take up her position, and passed Stiffman who had returned from the corridor; he was just off the phone from Pippa and had a sense of urgency about him.

"Listen up folks; they have scratched the feature about the missing ladder - apparently it's been found, so we are on air any minute. Places everyone please."

There was sudden increase in frenetic activity by the broadcast team; cameras were readied, people with oversized ear phones hunched over monitors and Stiffman's assistant appeared from nowhere to hand him an earpiece which he fixed in place. Silence fell over the band...

"We are live in three, two, one; Cue Cliff."

Stiffman took on a totally different personality as the red light went on, he thanked his co-host in the studio and facing the lead camera dead on, began their segment of the show.

"So here I am at Caramel Two studios with this bunch of talented, professional artistes as they embark on a twenty four hour gig-a-thon to raise some money..."

Bob had failed to mention this to anyone, so over the anchor-man's shoulder all viewers could see was a collection of grumpy musicians glaring at an old man, and as if this wasn't bad enough for Sophie, Stiffman had started to make his way towards the group while talking about the details of the event. As he passed her, a cold shiver ran down her spine - the man with the mic was heading towards the back of the band with a total disregard for what she had just said.

"Nooooo!" she screamed inside her head. "Where are you going?"

Stiffman reached the horn section.

"Let's catch up with a couple of the members..." he said as he reached Dr, Strange.

"Please, not him!" Sophie thought - his track record for weirdness was second to none and he looked decidedly awkward- clutching his trumpet as if it could go off at any moment.

"Hi, how long have you been playing?" Stiffman spoke into the mic, then pointed it in the doctor's direction for a response.

"Too many years to count, Cliff." said Strange with an air of confidence that Sophie never thought possible. She quickly assessed the situation and thought maybe he might just get away with it. Stiffman continued.

"And what would you say has been your biggest influence over this time?"

"Gravity." said the doctor.

With his follow up question, there was a flicker of alarm in Stiffmans voice; over the years as a professional broadcaster, his senses had become finely attuned to detect when a potential, career finishing nutter was in his presence.

"...and what about in music?"

"Chronologically; Stockhausen, Botticelli, and Bananarama." Replied Strange without missing a beat. The anchor-man's train of thought was thrown slightly as he processed the weird list; with his guard down he stepped outside of his professional remit for a moment to dispute the interviewee's comments.

"Surely Botticelli was a painter?"

Strange paused, then spoke with an affirming nod of the head.

"Oh yes, you're right..." Stiffman was satisfied the slip was just down to nerves and was on the brink of getting back on track when Strange continued. "...he did our downstairs hallway."

Luckily, Sophie was off camera – she loved misplaced humour and despite the seriousness of the situation couldn't help but find that amusing. The professional reporter carried on, but probably wished he hadn't.

"And why Stockhausen? Some may say he is a bit too avant-guard?"

"I liked the way he used contextual rhythms to contrast with a repetitive, melodic phrases..." He took a breath. "...and also the way he moved seamlessly from being the band's drummer to become the front man of Genesis."

Stiffman saw his career flash before his eyes, he had no idea where this loose cannon was going next, yet felt compelled to carry on talking to him.

"I think you`re getting confused with Phil Collins?"

"Oh, right." Strange didn't contest his conclusion; accepting that he probably knew more about showbiz than a lowly brain surgeon would. A tiny voice in Stiffmans ear shouting at him to stop talking to the idiot and move on, but his curiosity prevailed; he was determined to get at least one sensible answer from him.

"Any other music related influences?"

"Well, I have always been a big fan of Konrad Bartelski." came the matter of fact answer. Despite the heavy fake tan, Cliff was turning very pale.

"He was a downhill skier!" came the terse, un-professional retort.

"Well, obviously..." said Strange.

"Sorry?" said the weary interviewer.

"He could hardly have been an uphill skier, could he."

Stiffman was now resigned to the fact that this conversation wasn't going anywhere and edged down the line to talk to Bob.

"If I can move onto you sir, what's your name?"

"Hi, I'm Bob Marsh, owner of the studios."

Stiffman relaxed as he was now talking to a `normal`.

"Great, what are your..."

"We offer fantastic facilities at competitive prices..." Bob totally disregarded Stiffmans question and spoke over him, leaving the TV stalwart temporarily stunned; however he wasn't prepared for another nutter to ruin his day, so interrupted Bob to carry on with the interview.

"Terrific, so tell us why are you are all ..."

"...And we are open seven days a week."

The pair were soon locked into a game of verbal ping pong, each time one or the other spoke the volume of the conversation rose in order that the new front-runner could get their respective points across.

"How long have your band been..."

"…with discounts available for block bookings…" Bob sped up his delivery; he wanted to get as much advertising as possible, but sensed the mic could be removed any second. He needn't have worried; Stiffman was on the brink of giving up, knowing this probably was going to be his last ever interview.

"This is an ideal venue to meet other musos…" continued Bob, adding one final, throw-away line. "…and jam with top musicians like myself." He believed it sounded good and gave the studios a bit of gravitas, but Sophie knew different; admitting to be a professional player on live telly, whilst holding an instrument, probably wasn't going to end well. The seasoned journalist immediately jumped on it.

"You obviously have a lot of experience; have you played on any famous tracks?"

"No, not really." Bob now saw his error and started to back track knowing what was on the horizon; all he had to do was be calm and play down the `top trumpeter` angle and everything would be fine. Stiffman accepted this and was about to move on, when for some reason Doctor Strange interjected.

"He`s just being modest, he played with the Beatles once…"

Bob, who`s smile had now turned into a grimace threw a glance at Sophie, but there was nothing she could do; the cameras were rolling and every moment was being beamed across the airwaves.

"Wow, legendary stuff." Stiffman sensed a scoop; he was going to continue with the piece to camera when Strange interrupted again with more facts about Bob`s career.

"…and he was lead trumpet on the last four Bond themes." Then with a simple sentence, he took the farce to a whole new level. "…and I played second trumpet."

Bob was now experiencing a mix of emotions that ranged from utter embarrassment to apoplectic fury; a guy who he had only met a few times before in totally inexplicable circumstances, was now construction a lie so entwined around him, he had no way of escaping. And all on live TV. The eager journalist wasn't helping either…

"So you guys have been gigging together for years?" Stiffman bought the doctor back into the conversation.

"We go way back; remember the sessions we did for Tom Jones?" He began to reminisce, while Bob's stomach was turning summersaults.

"Oh good grief." he muttered, then he realised the camera was still pointed at him. "No, I mean yes..." he looked down at his shoes while he found a suitable phrase. "They were fun." He sounded very sheepish.

Stiffman was getting instructions from the director to wrap up and throw back to the studio.

"Well, in a few minutes we will hear the guys performing, which I think is going to be something special..." Sophie couldn't disagree with this sentiment, but for different reasons. "We are going to let the band finish their warm up and re-join them later for the start of their twenty-four hour marathon, meanwhile it's back to the studio."

The assistant confirmed they were clear from broadcast, and called Stiffman over to check his mic.

* * *

Bob was in a state of shock, his ambition for a bit of fun and marketing for the studio had drastically back fired; all he could do was stare at the ground, mulling over the previous conversation and contemplate the possible consequences of the next few minutes. His only chance of getting away with this lay with the proper musicians stood to his right - he had one hundred percent reliance on them to carry him through unscathed and with as much dignity intact as possible. Dr. Strange, on the other hand appeared to be totally oblivious to the impending social humiliation and was remarkably buoyant. He turned to Bob with a friendly, innocent smile.

"That was fun!"

This vexed Bob even further; rage and frustration coursed through his body and with a forced whisper, he snarled at the doctor.

"Why the hell did you say we are session musicians?" He awkwardly held up his trumpet. "Up until five minutes ago neither you nor I had the first clue which end of this lump of metal to blow down." Strange remained relaxed about the entire scenario.

"Don't worry, they can make us look good in the edit." Bob's grip around the trumpet tightened, his knuckles were almost translucent and teeth so firmly clenched his jaw practically locked.

"This is live TV!" he said, pointing out the obvious. The doctor paused and then calmly spoke.

"Can I offer you some advice? You should learn to relax; you're quite uptight and at your age you need to watch your blood pressure."

"I'm moments away from being asked to perform on live TV."

"Oh, I see." The doctor sounded sympathetic. "If I were you I would keep it simple, don't try anything too flash, maybe just stick to a simple melody."

Bob was shaking with anger and fear in equal measure.

"It's going to sound like a hamster farting into a dustbin."

Although being across the room and despite the ambient noise, Sophie understood every word Bob said. She felt sorry for him, and couldn't quite understand why Strange was being so antagonistic, then a thought struck her; perhaps the doctor was trying to help by causing a distraction, forcing her to think of others rather than herself - treatment by empathy: cure by compassion? It was an interesting viewpoint, unfortunately she didn't get a chance to explore it; Stiffman broke through the general hubbub with an announcement.

"Ok folks, I've just heard from the director, we are back on in a few minutes. Positions please."

These were words that Bob was dreading to hear; he kept telling himself all was going to be ok, but deep down he knew he was going to end up on one of those out-take shows. His anguished thoughts were broken by the trombone player; he had moved over to Bob's side to talk to him.

"Hi, I was just saying to my mate, it's always nice to meet a legendary player like yourself."

Bob's deception had gone too deep to back out now, so he kept up the pretence.

"I wouldn't expect too much tonight lads, I've got a bit of a sore throat, so was going to take it easy."

The saxophone player then piped up.

"I'm sure even on an off night, you will nail this."

"I was just saying, I've got a sore throat plus my lips are a bit tender; I'll probably lay off the high notes......and all the low ones too." Bob finished the sentence in his head.

"One minute everybody. Places please." Came the instruction from the assistant.

"What was it like playing with the Beatles?"

Bob really couldn't find the words to lie with anymore, so he tried to change the subject.

"Where do you guys normally play?"

"All over; we just turn up when we are told to."

"So, West-End musos? Session players?" Bob pressed for reassurance that all was going to be ok.

"Not really." replied the trombone player. This negative comment did nothing to allay Bob's fears; after all he was solely relying on these guys to get him through the next ten minutes. He needed a glimmer of hope from them; nervously Bob made another enquiry.

"So, where do you play then?"

Much to Bob's relief the trombone player turned to his colleague to clarify the last point.

"Actually, didn't you play in the West-End?"

"I did indeed." Bob was overwhelmed by this piece of news; it restored his sense of hope.

"That's great, which theatre?" said a relieved Bob

"Theatre? I was just by the ticket machine in Covent Garden tube - got moved on by the police."

Bob's face dropped a few inches.

"Thirty seconds folks. Stand by..."

They were nudging ever closer to going live, and Bob was now having palpitations; he desperately needed more time. A couple of minutes would be good, twenty years would be better so he could learn how to play the trumpet, but right now he would give anything to be elsewhere; even volunteer to go and move the sewers himself. He had one last shot at salvation.

"You chaps know what you are doing, right?" he asked the all-important question.

"Absolutely! No worries..." The trombone player broke off his final preparations to confirm with Bob, all was well.

"Great." was the only word Bob could find before the assistant call for total silence and started the ten second countdown to transmission. The trombone player leaned towards Bob and finished his sentence.

"...we just have to look good for the cameras." He quietly stated.

"WHAAAT!!?" shouted Bob at the top of his voice; the assistant glowered in their direction while counting in ever decreasing numbers. Bob didn't care by this point, he wanted to understand what his fellow brass player was talking about.

"What do you mean by that?" he roared through a forced whisper while his fellow horn player picked up his trombone and readied himself for the task ahead.

"Well, y'know, do all the moves in time with the music, that sort of thing."

"You do actually know how to play these horns, don't you?"

"Not really..." The sax player finally broke the news. "We are just hired to mime. Nick told us the professional players would cover the actual parts." He indicated to Bob and Strange. "That's you guys, right?"

"Mime artists! I was told you boys were ex Top of the Pops... wait a minute."

As he spoke the realization dawned on him, Bob could now see where the confusion lay. Under normal circumstances he would probably have been mildly amused, even taken a small amount of pleasure by some poor sod finding themselves in a tricky situation. However, he was that poor sod and time had run out.

"Three, two, one..." As the assistant launched the live transmission, Bob felt faint and slunk into a nearby chair, hoping for some miracle to be performed to prevent the next four minutes from happening.

"A power cut, maybe?" he muttered to himself, but the lights stayed on. "Stiffman struck down by a rare tropical disease?" He looked at the newsman now speaking into the camera; he remained upright and with a healthy glow.

"Alien invasion?" He gave a quick glance at the door urging a troupe of green blobs to squelch their way in and take over earth. Nothing.

"Maybe this is all just a bad dream..."

* * *

Chapter 11

Sophie lay on the bed; still. Her life support machine, the only constant in her life at the moment continued with its monotonous, relentless beeping noise.

"I'm going to turn that damned thing off one day; even if it's the last thing I do..."

Sophie chuckled to herself, having a sense of humour had kept her buoyant during the recent, dark days – the curious dreamscapes and absurd scenarios of an overactive mind had kept her from dwelling on the desperate thoughts of her predicament. However, now it was time to go home - Sophie was desperate to see her family and return to the frenetic, disordered, normal life that she always complained about.

A new noise, one she hadn't heard before, appeared on her aural horizon; a slow, regular clicking that irritated her slightly as it didn't quite fit in with the rhythmical beep of her machine - she urged the tapping to speed up to keep time. Suddenly it stopped; just outside her door. Doctor Strange who, unbeknown to Sophie was already by her bedside, spoke.

"Hi, how's the foot doing?"

"Not too bad today." Said Sophie`s mum. "I'm getting used to the crutches. She hobbled through the door and sat on the end of Sophie`s bed. "How is she today, Doctor?"

"Well, I do believe she has made a transition in the last few hours; without boring you with too many technical details, the monitor has shown an increase in brain activity - which is a positive." The doctor produced some charts from among his paperwork. "If we look at the period between eleven this morning and four in the afternoon, the readout shows a steady increase; then at around five o'clock, for about an hour the needle almost jumped off the scale. I'm not sure what she was thinking about at this time, but it must have been incredibly motivating." He smiled and indicated to Sophie's head. "It's like she was having a party in there."

Mum smiled, it was reassuring to hear, as this was a belief she had all along. Sophie was listening to the conversation and had to agree; the last few days had been incredible - experiencing one of the most famous battles in British history as her all-time naval hero had been fascinating; spending time among the captured airmen of Stalag Luft had left her feeling humbled, and watching Bob make a complete twit of himself on live T.V made up for all the duff gigs he had sent them on. Despite being comatose, life was good!

"Hi, Mum." A voice sounded from the doorway, Knobby walked in, closely followed by Johnson. "How's sis today?"

"The doctor was just saying, it looks like she has made some great improvements."

"That's good news." Sophie's brother went over to the bed and gave his mum a quick hug.

"What have you been up to?" she asked.

"We just finished a jam at the studio, thought we would pop in." replied Knobby as Johnson found a space to stand in.

"Everyone at college sends their best." He spoke softly. "We all miss her." his message had a personal sentiment attached.

* * *

Sophie lay reflecting on recent days; she recognised her body was enduring a great trauma and the long term effects were yet to be realised, but despite the adversity she remained positive. The imaginary worlds created by her fanciful mind had provided a safe haven away from the turmoil and duress of the physical ailment and to Sophie's thinking, a light was still on and someone was definitely at home.

The conversation in the room flowed at a gentle pace and for a few moments the chatter weaved its way in and out of her consciousness with the same hypnotic qualities of a babbling brook. Her mum spoke with Johnson about college and the Doctor updated her brother. Then, a thought suddenly struck her.

"Now would be a great time to wake up!"

Although being in a coma had been enlightening, she was ready to surrender the power to transcend time, dictate situations she had created and return to normality. But how - was the burning question.

"Why am I asleep? What is it that is keeping me here?"

They were two very good questions that had far reaching consequences; just making this simple enquiry somehow triggered an inherent reaction – a basic survival instinct, deep inside her brain. A previously inaccessible portion of her mind suddenly unlocked and synapses that had been dormant, fired back into life sending pulses of information across cells and onwards throughout her body. Slowly but surely some of her senses came back on line; she become aware of her mum's presence on her bed, pressing down on the blanket which in turn placed pressure across her legs; the sensor that clamped around her index finger suddenly become uncomfortable as she felt it restrict her blood flow.

"I can feel my pulse!"

It was a simple sensation which she always took for granted, but now was the most exhilarating feeling Sophie had felt for a while.

* * *

But, as her self-awareness grew, so did her internal perception; a heavy weight bore down on her mind, and created an increasing pressure that in turn restricted her physical qualities; movement, sight, rational thought. Sophie had sensed this entity all along, but didn't know what shape it was. The boulder-like object had come to rest across her brain and had cast a long, dark shadow over her being.

"That's why I'm getting bloody headaches, and... " She paused to absorb the notion that had just struck her. "This rock is my coma." Sophie had no idea that her illness would have a physical form, and yet there it was - granite like in appearance, the element had a rugged surface with thousands of tiny holes all over. Despite its dense form, it was soft to touch and unusually cold. Sophie didn't know from which part of her vast mind it had derived from; all she knew was to survive it needed to be elevated from her head to relieve the ever growing pressure.

* * *

The stone was large and cumbersome and would be tricky to handle - it's diameter was much larger than her arm span, so any attempt to shift this dead-weight was not going to be easy. With a gargantuan effort she started to raise the enormity of its mass upwards, but every time she managed to get a purchase on one end, the other started to tilt downwards and overbalanced her. Reacting quickly she readjusted her stance to increase the upward thrust and maintain the status quo - she tried again, this time it rose a few, vital millimetres.

This action of the weight being alleviated from Sophie's head, albeit by a fraction, had a very positive effect; with the blockage partly removed, fresh life coursed through her body and her senses started to function again. There were now the thinnest slivers of light penetrating through to her pupils, and Sophie's sense of smell detected the tiniest hint of an aroma she recognised as `hospital` - normally a detested odour, but now she welcomed it with open nostrils. It was a clear signal that her journey back to a normal life had started. All she had to do was completely remove the weight from her head.

Steeling herself for another attempt she took three deep breaths, with each one her muscles tensed in readiness for the strain they were about to experience. With an almighty and determined thrust, Sophie's legs heaved upwards, her arms locked in positon and she was able to shift the obstruction further than before. Straining under its bulk, the compression surrounding Sophie's head began to ebb away and her mind starting whirring and ticking over - juddering at first as the cogs started to warm up. Thousands of dormant thoughts and memories that had been trapped beneath the seemingly immovable object, suddenly came tumbling out. Small, wispy packages of mind-data floated randomly around like snowflakes in a flurry, and with childlike wonderment her immediate instinct was to try and catch one as it floated past.

Her hand shot out and gently scooped up the nearest memory, but as she cradled it in her palm trying not to crush it, her balance became unstable and the load above her head started to drop back down. The rock descended very slowly at first, disobeying the normal laws of physics, but this afforded Sophie enough time to have a quick glance at the memory in her hand. She froze. Out of all the memories that were drifting about her headspace, the one she had salvaged was her very earliest recollection; a childhood Christmas with the family. She couldn't let that go - it was too precious. The weight above her started to gain downward momentum and Sophie's arm quickly grew tired; she stated to panic.

"No! I'm getting better!" she yelled at herself. "I can hear conversations; I can see light; I can smell cleaning fluids..."

Sophie struggled further; the more she tried to raise its hefty bulk, the greater the resistance it supplied, almost as if her expelled energy was being absorbed by the porous surface, feeding the dead weight - making it stronger and heavier.

Time passed – the battle continued and the tipping point of no return was rapidly approaching; the rock like object that had been acting like an anchor on Sophie's mind, trapping her in a dark place, was once again about to enforce all of its might upon her will.

"NOOOO!" She tried to fight back with all her strength, determined to remove the one thing standing between her and freedom from the coma. With one final explosion of energy - the last ounce she could muster, Sophie raised the weight back to where it was... but no further; she had just enough power to counteract the object's mass, but not to remove it completely. It was deadlock. She began to cry.

* * *

"What's the matter Soph?" said a voice behind her.

She froze; to suddenly hear someone speak from within the darkness was terrifying; her heart raced and muscles burned as she strained under the weight; the pressure in her head was reaching dangerous limits – there was no safety valve and every blood soaked pulse that throbbed through her skull created further disorientation. She craned her head round to see who had spoken; out from the corner of one teary eye she saw a blurred figure standing nearby, but didn't know who it was. Tears started to flow with more potency – with every drop shed the weight above inched back down towards her skull, it was almost as if her sobbing was washing the last of her strength away. Sophie had come so close to freedom but she knew the battle was lost. The rock closed in.

"I can't do this anymore!" she screamed. "I just want to go home."

Her emotions were now uncontrollable and as the black shadow descended over her once again, she resigned herself to the fate she once hoped could be avoided. The senses that had started to revive, began to fade back to obscurity; Sophie was now at her lowest point and genuinely believed that she was soon to become a part of history herself.

She closed her eyes and waited for the inevitable.

* * *

The darkness shrouded Sophie and she retracted further into its claustrophobic depths, the rock constantly pressing down causing her to slowly sink into oblivion. She started to count in descending seconds to gracefully signify the last moments and bring her life to an orderly close.

"Ten, nine, eight, seven..."

The rock stopped. Its unrelenting journey had been completed; with eyes still closed tightly, Sophie braced herself for its next move; it could be a sudden crushing sensation, or maybe this was it...

"...Three, two, one..."

The boulder remained still for what seemed like an eternity, as if to taunt her; Sophie relaxed, there was nothing more she could do.

Without warning the enormous weight suddenly reversed its direction and gradually started to lift up, away from Sophie's head, which in turn immediately eased the pressure on her skull. Quickly, she opened her eyes and desperately tried to focus; a hazy light now fought pass the ascending rock, cutting through the darkness, illuminating a figure before her. It was Bob, standing in plain sight, arms outstretched baring the enormity of her burden; he didn't struggle with the massive weight, but merely supported the load which allowed Sophie to move without any further interference. He looked at her with a warm and caring expression, one that she hadn't seen from him for a long time.

"Is that better?" he asked. The stress on Sophie's head was now receding at a fantastic rate and her senses revived their normal functions; By now, Bob took all the weight of the rock and Sophie was able to remove her aching hands from aloft, wipe tears away from her eyes and take a small, but significant step forward, away from the shade and into the light. Through bleary eyes she looked directly at Bob and smiled back at him; she went to talk but choked by emotion the words caught in her throat, instead she mouthed the sincere and heartfelt message.

"Thank you, dad."

Still supporting the rock, he began to well up, but managed to hide his sentiment with a well-timed wink and nod of the head.

"Off you go, love; take care." said Bob.

* * *

Sophie's room was now crowded; Bob had joined the others around ten minutes ago having received a call from the ward sister; the message was vague in detail, but he understood enough to know that Sophie's condition was changing and he should be present.

Currently, he sat opposite her mum holding Sophie's hand tightly, but looking at his estranged wife. Although their relationship had been strained for a while, differences were put aside as they focused on the one thing that united them – Sophie's condition. Despite their daughter's brain presenting an outwardly vacant status, both were adamant that, on some level her mind remained fully functioning in its natural, vibrant way; and they were right. Basic tasks were being looked after by the beeping machine, but in the gaps between the whirring cogs that formed the hidden side of Sophie's consciousness - humorous notions and philosophies acted as lubricants, keeping her mind agile and the tinniest, but vital spark of life, alive.

* * *

Sophie slowly roamed down one of the many corridors that formed her mind. She began to cry again, but this time because of relief and understanding, rather than suppression and frustration; with every tentative step she took towards the glowing light and away from the depressive, bleak shadow cast by the rock, she felt the coma was slowly releasing her from its vice like grip.

Sophie lay on the bed. Still...

The End

Printed in Great Britain
by Amazon

31144993R00088